Escape From Odd Island

A HUGO DARE ADVENTURE

DAVID CODD

PROLOGUE

I started to run.

I figured I had about one minute to escape. One minute before they set off after me. One minute starting from now.

Sixty ... fifty-nine ... fifty-eight ...

I quickly picked up the pace. I had been told there was a forest out there so that was what I aimed for. I hoped the trees would provide some kind of cover and maybe they would have. Unfortunately, there seemed to be something preventing me from ever reaching them.

And that *something* was fog.

The thickest, densest, most *foggiest* fog I had ever encountered.

Forty-nine ... forty-eight ... forty-seven ...

I tried to ignore it, but the fog was everywhere I turned. Left, right and centre. Above and below. Up close and personal. Whether I liked it or not, I simply couldn't avoid it.

And I couldn't avoid tripping over my own feet either. Running at full pelt, my left hit my right before a combination of the two sent the rest of me tumbling. I hit the ground hard and rolled over. It hurt, but there was no time to feel sorry for myself. If I was going to escape then I had to keep moving. The minute (like most minutes tend to do) was disappearing fast. Which reminds me …

Thirty-five … thirty-four … thirty-three …

Oh, will you please stop counting, Hugo? It's really not helping.

That's me in case you're wondering. Hugo Dare. Agent Minus Thirty-Five. Codename Pink Weasel, but you can call me Pinky. I'm a spy, but, on this particular occasion, I had seen enough to last a lifetime. Still, it wasn't as if things could get any worse.

One howl later, however, and I realised they could.

I had been warned about the wild wolves. How they stalked the compound and hunted their prey in packs. Now they were closing in. Getting ready to strike.

And I don't think I need to tell you who they were targeting!

Fear overwhelmed me and I kicked out in panic. My foot failed to connect with anything wolf-like, but I kicked out again. Better to be safe than sorry.

Twenty-two … twenty-one … twenty …

Scrambling up off the ground, I tried to put the wolves to the back of my mind as I pressed on wearily into the gloom. Where was the forest? Surely I should've reached it by now.

Ten … nine … eight …

I was slowing down. Sensing my weakness, the fog seemed to wrap itself around my body, squeezing the life out of me before I could resist. I carried on for a few more steps before I began to stagger. There was no end in sight, but I had reached the end regardless.

Escaping was never meant to be this hard.

Five … four … three …

I was still two seconds shy of the full minute when my legs gave way from under me. To say I was tired was an understatement. I was beyond exhausted. Completely drained. An empty shell of a boy.

The howling may have come to an end, but now a shrill, high-pitched screech-like feedback from a speaker was trying its best to fill the silence. Coming from somewhere above me, it wasn't long before that, too, stopped suddenly, only to be replaced by a voice.

'Well, that didn't go to plan now, did it?' giggled a man.

No. Obviously not.

'Rules are there for a reason,' he continued. 'I am to be obeyed at all times. Do you understand that now, my child? Has it finally sunk in?'

I curled up into a ball, beaten and defeated. I had let myself down. No, it was worse than that. Much, much worse. I had let the others down, too.

Dodge.

Mo.

Wheelie.

Angel.

They were my friends. I had promised them I would escape and yet I had failed at the first attempt. Maybe that was it. No more second chances. What if we were doomed to spend the rest of our lives with the strangest man we had ever had the misfortune to meet?

What if we were stuck on Odd Island forever?

1.'THERE'S SOMEBODY ELSE DOWN HERE.'

Let's rewind the clock a little.

Three days, sixteen hours and thirty-seven minutes to be precise. Wow, that really is precise. I don't know how I do it sometimes. (Truth is, I don't. I make most of it up as I go along, but nobody ever seems to notice.)

It was a Sunday morning in winter. Not so early that my eyes refused to open, but early enough that I had been forced to skip breakfast as I hurried out of the house. If I'm being honest, I was too excited to eat anyway. Not only had I been summoned to Slippery Simon's Swimming Spectacular, but I had been summoned at short notice. And, as everybody knows, there's only one reason you get summoned to Slippery Simon's at short notice ... and that's to go swimming. Makes sense, right?

Apparently not.

'Let me get this straight,' I sighed. 'We're not actually going swimming, are we?'

'Of course we're not, you blithering buffoon,' barked the

Big Cheese. He was the chief of secret spy organisation, SICK, and the man I called boss. He also looked remarkably like a walrus, but that's a story for another time. 'We're spies, young Dare,' he continued. 'The clue is in the name. We spy. What in the wild world of weirdness made you think we'd be going swimming?'

'*You* did.' I gestured at the queue of people that had gathered behind me. 'I put two and two together when you told me to meet you here and came up with a super splashy Sunday. This is the only water-based theme park in the whole of Crooked Elbow. It's got slides ... well, *a* slide ... and a diving board ... also known as a plank of wood ... not to mention talking seals on surfboards ... okay, so that last bit might be a slight exaggeration—'

'Is that why you've turned up in just your trunks?' asked Poppy Wildheart, looking me up and down. Both wide-eyed and even wider mouthed, she was the Big Cheese's personal assistant (as well as my own personal favourite on the spy scene).

I wrapped my arms around my half-naked body and tried not to shiver. 'Maybe.'

'You always were a silly little sausage, young Dare,' groaned the Big Cheese, shaking his moustache at me.

'Don't be too harsh on him, sir,' insisted Poppy. 'It was a simple mistake to make. Now, let's see what we can find for him to wear. Starting with these ...' Poppy handed me a pair of green plastic flip-flops. 'They'll come in handy where you're going,' she said, much to my confusion. 'What about you, sir? Have you got anything you can lend Agent Minus

Thirty-Five to warm him up a little?'

'I wouldn't have thought so,' shrugged the Big Cheese. 'I wear all my clothes for a reason … and that reason is to keep me nice and toasty. Even now I'm dressed in two coats … two waistcoats … two shirts … and two pairs of trousers. I've even been known to stretch to three pairs of socks when it's really chilly. A lot like today, in fact.'

'One thing will do, sir,' pressed Poppy.

'Well, as I'm feeling generous …' The Big Cheese carefully removed the thin silk cravat from around his neck. 'Try not to lose it,' he said, frowning at me as he reluctantly handed it over. 'I've only got another seventy-four at home. Nowhere near enough to just give away. Right, enough of this idle chitter-chatter. The only way for young Dare to keep out the cold is by getting down to business.' With that, the Big Cheese tapped a suede loafer on the manhole cover beneath his feet. 'Down below business,' he said, winking at me.

My shoulders slumped as it suddenly dawned on me why I had been summoned. Yes, I was going to get wet … but not in the way I was hoping.

'I'm not doing it,' I blurted out. 'No way. If nothing else, it stinks!'

'Then that's something you both have in common,' said the Big Cheese rudely.

'I might smell … but I don't smell *that* bad!' I argued.

The Big Cheese threw his arms up in irritation. 'It's only a sewer.'

'Only a sewer?' I repeated, horrified. 'Would you go down there, sir?'

7

'Me?' Tipping back his head, the Big Cheese roared with laughter. 'Of course not, young Dare! I'm far too important for such nonsense. Only a complete numpty brain would even consider going down into a sewer.'

Yes, I know what that makes me. And, no, you don't have to rub it in. I have got feelings, you know.

'Why me, sir?' I moaned.

'Why not you?' replied the Big Cheese awkwardly.

'That's not really an answer, sir,' said Poppy, chipping in. 'Maybe Hugo would prefer it if you told him that he's one of our finest agents ... the ideal spy for the mission at hand ... and ... erm ... lots of other nice things that roll smoothly off your tongue.'

'But that would be bending the truth, Miss Wildheart,' said the Big Cheese. 'Bending it to such a point that it shatters. No, I chose young Dare because he's small and – no offence intended – stupid enough to do as he's told. The perfect combination under the circumstances.'

'You say the sweetest things, sir,' I muttered under my breath. 'One last question though, before I go wandering about in the sewer. What's down there?'

'Not what ... *who*,' said the Big Cheese, correcting me.

'And that who is Deadly De'Ath,' revealed Poppy.

I shivered as she spoke. This, however, it had nothing to do with my obvious lack of clothing and everything to do with the name she had just uttered. Deadly De'Ath was the criminal kingpin of Crooked Elbow. SICK's number one nemesis. The baddest of the bad guys.

'We're one hundred and seven per-cent certain that

De'Ath is hiding out beneath our very feet,' the Big Cheese remarked. 'Well … *probably* certain.'

'Probably?' It was funny how a single word could set my alarm bells ringing. 'You can't be probably certain, sir.'

'You probably certainly can if I say so,' insisted the Big Cheese. 'Besides, we have witnesses.'

'That's not strictly true, sir,' said Poppy, chipping in for a second time. 'We have *a* witness. And even she was half asleep on a moving bus when she saw someone suspicious fiddling with the manhole cover.'

'Someone suspicious?' I screwed up my face. 'You mean it could have been anyone?'

'No, it could not have been anyone,' argued the Big Cheese. 'It had to be *someone*. And that someone *was* Deadly De'Ath. For your information, young Dare, we've been monitoring this manhole cover for the past five days.'

'Five days?' I gasped. 'That's a long time to watch a manhole cover.'

'Yes … well … maybe not five *whole* days exactly,' mumbled the Big Cheese, refusing to look me in the eye. 'To clarify, Agent Seventeen travels this way to work, Agent Twenty-One passes here on his way home, and Agent Forty-Six has been known to occasionally walk his dog around these parts. That's good enough for me.'

'Of course it is,' I said, rolling my eyes. 'That's more like five minutes than five days.'

'Okay, clever-clogs,' frowned the Big Cheese, 'tell me this. If you were Deadly De'Ath, where would you hide out?'

'Not in a sewer, that's for sure,' I said. 'Somewhere

secluded probably … in the middle of nowhere. Like a … lighthouse!'

'A lighthouse?' nodded Poppy. 'Good thinking.'

'Is it?' The Big Cheese turned away from me. 'Miss Wildheart, send an agent to check on every lighthouse in Crooked Elbow,' he whispered. 'There's only one so it shouldn't take too long. As for you, young Dare,' he said, tapping his foot for a second time, 'your sewer awaits. Don't look like that; you can come out after ten minutes. No, make that eleven. Not so obvious.'

'What happens after eleven minutes?' I wondered.

'We're going to flood the sewer,' revealed the Big Cheese, rubbing his hands together. 'We've got a big hose. It's on its way now. Probably best not to hang around too long once we get started. Right, if you'll do the honours please, Miss Wildheart …'

Crouching down, Poppy used both hands to shift the manhole cover to one side. 'You're right about the pong,' she said, backing away. 'It is a bit whiffy down there.'

'A *bit* whiffy?' I groaned. 'I think you'll find it's a proper stinkfest. An absolute smell hole.'

'Don't let that put you off,' insisted the Big Cheese. 'Now, have you got your torch?'

'What torch?' I shrugged. 'Surely you don't mean the torch you didn't tell me to bring when you also didn't tell me that I wasn't going swimming?'

'I've got a torch,' said Poppy, passing it to me. I shoved it down the front of my trunks for safe-keeping before I took to the steps that led down into the sewer. I had almost disappeared from view when Poppy spoke again. 'Now remember, Hugo, you're only there to observe. Catching De'Ath yourself is not an option. It's far too dangerous. We've got other agents who can do that.'

'*Skilled* agents,' added the Big Cheese.

'He means agents with different skills to you,' said Poppy swiftly. 'Good luck, Hugo. Ten minutes, that's all.'

'Eleven,' said the Big Cheese, correcting her.

Poppy smiled wearily as I ducked down below the surface of the earth. With that, she moved the manhole cover back into place until, inch by inch, I was plunged into an all-consuming darkness.

I took a breath and continued down the steps, all the while trying desperately not to think about what I had let myself in for. I stopped when I reached the bottom and removed the torch. Knowing my luck, it wouldn't even work when I flicked it on.

And yet it did.

Ah, that was better. I moved the light around and cast an eye over my surroundings. As far as I could tell the sewer consisted of a narrow tunnel with damp walls and puddles of water beneath my feet. It did smell pretty revolting down there, but nowhere near as bad as I had imagined. Maybe the Big Cheese knew a thing or two about sewers, after all. He had to know something I suppose.

Pointing the torch away from the steps, I set off along the tunnel as quickly as Poppy's flip-flops would allow. I thought I was moving fast until I spied something else moving much faster beside me. It was down in the water, scampering between my feet. My first thought was that it was a rat, whilst every thought thereafter was an attempt to convince myself that my eyes were playing tricks on me.

With my mind pre-occupied with all things rodent-like, it took me a while to notice that the tunnel was bending ever so slightly to my left. Beyond that, there was another light. I watched as it bounced off the walls, edging closer with every passing second.

Somebody was coming.

I turned off my own torch for fear of being spotted. With no obvious hiding place available, I crouched down in the darkness and made myself as small as possible. I gasped as the icy water soaked into my trunks. Nervous that my next gasp might be even louder, I stuck a hand over my mouth and waited.

It wasn't long before I heard a voice.

'There's somebody else down here.'

My heart leapt up into my mouth. I knew who it was. That's the good news.

The bad news is I'm not going to tell you until the next chapter.

2.'YOU'RE NOT AS MISERABLE AS YOU LIKE TO MAKE OUT.'

It wasn't Deadly De'Ath in the sewer if that's what you're thinking.

No, it *was* Layla Krool. She was De'Ath's second in command. His number two. His right-hand woman. Which made Krool not quite as vile as De'Ath himself, but still at least thirteen times more horrible than your average Crooked criminal.

I guessed she wasn't alone. Not unless she was talking to herself. Which was always possible I suppose, especially if she'd been stuck in the sewer for as long as the Big Cheese seemed to imagine.

A second voice, however, answered that particular question.

'There's nobody else down here, Auntie Layla. Only you and me ... me and you ... you and me again. I'm so bored I could probably fall asleep whilst talking to you. Wake me up if I do. No, on second thoughts, don't bother!'

Oh, you've got to be joking!

I knew instantly who the second voice belonged to … and just as instantly wished I didn't! Her name was Fatale De'Ath and we had history. Not only was she Deadly De'Ath's unpredictably dangerous daughter, but we were also friends. Kind of. It's hard to explain so I don't think I'll bog you down with the details. Let's just say that we had saved each other's lives on more than one occasion. Now we were equal, though. And seeing as I was on the side of the good guys and she wasn't, then I suppose it also meant that we were enemies.

'Auntie?' Layla Krool drew a long, weary breath. 'Do not call me that, Miss De'Ath. I am not your auntie.'

'No, but you could always be my mum,' suggested Fatale. 'That job's up for grabs if you fancy it. My dad wouldn't mind. You think he's super evil and he thinks you're … um … pretty … pretty nasty, I mean. That should be enough for the two of you to go and get married. Kissy-wissy-woo and all that nonsense!'

'Not this again,' groaned Krool.

'Oh, am I repeating myself?' laughed Fatale. 'What do you expect? We have been stuck down here for four days now—'

'Five,' said Krool, correcting her.

'Five?' cried Fatale. 'It's even worse than I thought. Just remind me. When can we leave again?'

Krool replied without missing a beat. 'Soon.'

'You said that yesterday,' moaned Fatale. 'And the day before that. And you'll probably say it again tomorrow if we're still down here. I just want to go above ground and have some fun.'

'Your father doesn't like you going above ground,' shot back Krool. 'And he certainly doesn't like you having fun. That's why he's left you with me whilst he's off searching for a new hideout.'

'You're not as miserable as you like to make out,' remarked Fatale.

'I think you'll find I am,' insisted Krool. 'I'm a very miserable person. Miserable *and* angry. And you may have seen me miserable, but you wouldn't want to see me angry.'

'At least it wouldn't be boring,' sighed Fatale. The sewer fell silent for what felt like an eternity, but was probably no more than a few seconds. 'Have you heard from my dad yet?' Fatale asked eventually.

'No,' replied Krool, 'but then I don't expect to either. He'll return when he's ready. We just have to be patient. I hope that's not going to be a problem ...'

Fatale snorted loudly. 'I can do patient. No, I'm being serious. I'm a very patient person. Maybe I'll just run along now and ... erm ... play with the rats for the rest of the day. I hope that's patient enough for you ... *auntie.*'

I waited for Krool to reply, but it never came. So, that was that then. Conversation over. Listening carefully, I heard the splatter of footsteps through the puddles. The sound slowly faded and I guessed that both Fatale and Layla Krool were heading back the way they had come. They were moving away from me.

I left it a few seconds before I stood up. Then I left it a few more before I pointed the torch back towards the steps. I had heard it with my own ears; Deadly De'Ath was above ground searching for a new hideout. Which meant there was no need for me to hang around a moment longer.

I flicked the switch, but the torch refused to shine. Frustrated, I shook it twice and the light flashed on and off in quick succession. The anger was starting to build by now so I smacked it against my hand. Nothing happened. I smacked it again and this time the torch slipped out of my grasp, landing somewhere between my feet with a *splash*.

Well done, Hugo. Very clever.

I took a breath and tried to compose myself. Okay, so I couldn't see a thing, but there was no need to panic. Not yet, anyway. All I had to do was make my way back towards the steps. If I remembered correctly it was practically a straight line. How hard could it actually be?

I found out one step later when I walked blindly into a wall. No, my mistake. This was softer than a wall. Soft like human flesh.

Soft like a girl.

I screwed up my face as a bright light hit me fair and square between the eyes.

'Wotcha', Stinky, fancy seeing you down here.'

3.'I THOUGHT YOU WERE A SPY.'

Fatale De'Ath took hold of my shoulders and shook me until my eyeballs began to rattle.

'This is a nice surprise,' she cried. 'I've missed you so much.'

'You've got a funny way of showing it,' I moaned. I shuffled backwards until her hands fell away. 'Now turn that light off. I don't want Krool to see it.'

'Don't get your trunks in a twist about Auntie Layla,' insisted Fatale, lowering the torch. 'She'll have wandered up the other end of the sewer by now. She likes to keep a distance between us. Don't ask me why, but I think I irritate her.' Fatale grabbed my cheeks and squeezed them together. 'I don't irritate you though, do I, Stinky? We're as tight as a … erm … tightrope. I can't believe you're here. I haven't seen you for ages. When was the last time we met? Let me think …'

'There's no need,' I said. 'I can remember it clearly. It was when your father tried to kill me.'

'Ah, so it was,' mumbled Fatale, pulling a face at me.

I took a moment to look her up and down. She was wearing

a long white dress with ruffles and bows and all manner of other twiddly bits. Totally unsuitable for a sewer of course, but then Fatale had no doubt worn it for that exact reason.

'You don't normally spend your Sundays underground,' she said suspiciously. 'What are you doing here, Stinky? You're not searching for my father, are you?'

'Your father?' I spluttered. 'Why would I be searching for your father?'

'I don't know …. maybe because it's all you ever do!' grumbled Fatale. 'Yes, I am fully aware that he's only just escaped from prison, but that doesn't give you the right to make his life a misery. Sometimes I think I'm the only person who really likes him. Oh, and Auntie Layla, of course. They'd make a sweet couple, don't you think?'

'Yeah, lovely,' I said, shaking my head. 'A real gruesome twosome. Listen, this has been … erm … enjoyable, but it's probably time I … whoa!'

My sentence was cut short as Fatale pressed her forearm against my throat, pinning me to the wall of the sewer. 'I like you, Stinky,' she began. 'You're my best friend. Well, my only friend. Well, the only kid I know who's about my age and isn't terrified of me. No, that didn't come out right. I'll start again, shall I? I like you, Stinky, but I won't betray my father. Not now, not ever. So, I'll ask you again. What are you doing in the sewer?'

I didn't reply. Not because I didn't want to, but because I couldn't. With Fatale's arm still pressed against my throat, I could barely breathe, let alone speak. Not that Fatale seemed to realise this.

'Have it your way,' she shrugged. 'Maybe you'd rather talk to Auntie Layla ...'

The pressure eased as Fatale spun away, ready to shout for Krool. Free to move, I reached up with both hands and pulled on her pigtails.

'Ow!' Fatale squealed. 'What did you do that for?'

'I couldn't breathe,' I gasped.

'And?' replied Fatale stubbornly.

'And that's not a good thing,' I said, stating the obvious. 'If I can't breathe, I can't speak. And if I can't speak then I can't tell you why I'm here.'

'Oh, is that how it works?' snorted Fatale. 'Go on then. Tell me.'

Whoops. I had forgotten about that bit. It wasn't as if I could tell her the truth (even if she had already guessed correctly). 'I'm ... I'm ...'

'Don't lie to me, Stinky,' warned Fatale.

'As if I would,' I said innocently. 'I'm a ... a ... a sewer inspector!'

Wow. Where did that come from? My mouth, yes, but certainly not my brain.

'A sewer inspector?' repeated Fatale. 'Did you really just say that?'

'So it seems.' I had started now so I would have to finish. 'It's my new job,' I blurted out. 'Weekends only, of course. When I'm not at school. The Crooked Council send me down into the sewers so I can ... inspect them.'

Fatale refused to take her eyes off me. I don't know why, but it was almost as if she didn't believe what I was saying.

'What are you looking for when you inspect them?' she asked.

'Good question.' I stopped talking and ran a hand over the wall beside me. 'I normally just check that they're still … you know … *sewery*.'

'I don't think *sewery* is a word,' frowned Fatale.

'Maybe not to you,' I said smugly, 'but then you're not like me. You're not a sewer inspector.'

'I thought you were a spy,' pressed Fatale.

I shrugged. 'Spy … sewer inspector … they're much the same thing when you think about it.'

'I've thought about it and they're not,' argued Fatale. 'And there's something else I don't understand either. I asked you what you were doing in the sewer, but you never asked me. Not once. Don't you think that's a little strange. It's almost as if you were expecting to find me down here.'

I screwed up my face. There was no point pretending anymore. Fatale had me rumbled and there was no getting out of it.

I was about to own up and tell her the truth when Fatale beat me to it. 'Can you hear that?' she asked, tilting her head towards the steps.

'Oh, that was me.' I struggled not to blush as I rubbed my stomach. 'Sometimes they just escape by accident—'

'Not that,' said Fatale, pressing a hand over my mouth. 'Listen properly. Can you hear it now?'

I tried to speak, but Fatale didn't seem interested in what I had to mumble.

'Shush,' she said. 'It's getting louder. It sounds like … water.'

I forcefully removed her hand so I could finally answer. 'We are in a sewer. The two do tend to go hand in hand.'

'No, this is more than just drips and drops,' Fatale insisted. 'This is the sound of running water ... like a river ... gushing towards us.'

'Why would there be a river gushing towards—?' I stopped suddenly as the memories came flooding back. *Literally* flooding back.

The Big Cheese had set me an eleven minute time limit before they got busy with their hose.

I hadn't been counting, but I guessed that those same eleven minutes were up.

4.'I THINK I WOULD LIKE TO RUN NOW.'

Fatale De'Ath clenched her fist and knocked on my forehead.

'What's wrong?' she asked.

'Nothing,' I lied. 'Not really. Except … *now* might be a good time to start running. And fast. Would you like me to lead the way?'

I pulled on Fatale's arm, but she refused to budge. 'Why are we running?'

'No reason.' I glanced back over my shoulder towards the steps. I could hear it myself now. It was coming up behind us. 'Well, there is *one* reason,' I admitted. 'A *wet* reason.'

'Tell me more,' demanded Fatale.

I let go of her and started to run. 'They're flooding the sewers.'

'Who are?' asked Fatale, more confused than ever as she set off after me.

'The Crooked Council,' I replied without thinking.

'And why would the Crooked Council want to flood the

sewers?' Fatale was already out in front and I was trailing behind, struggling to keep up. I could've blamed the flip-flops but, given the chance, the flip-flops would probably have blamed me. Still, at least I wasn't hindered by any loose clothing. Or *any* clothing come to that. 'Stinky, answer my question!' cried Fatale. 'Why would the Crooked Council want to flood the sewers?'

'No, they're not flooding them,' I remarked. 'My mistake. They're ... um ... washing them. They always give the sewers a good spring clean around this time of year.'

'A spring clean?' repeated Fatale. 'In winter?'

'They like to start early,' I explained. 'Or late. I'll let you decide.' I looked along the length of the tunnel and saw movement in the distance. 'Is that who I think it is?'

'Only if you think it's Auntie Layla,' replied Fatale. Right on cue, a light shone straight at us. 'Don't do that,' Fatale moaned, covering her eyes.

A bewildered Layla Krool slowly lowered her torch. 'What's going on, Miss De'Ath?' she asked. 'Who's that with you? No ... it can't be ... not Pink Weasel!'

'Run,' shouted Fatale, racing towards her. 'I'll explain later.'

'You'll explain now,' said Krool firmly. 'And stop calling me—'

'Run,' I echoed. 'Run ... run ... run.'

'And *you* definitely don't tell me what to do, Weasel boy,' Krool spat.

Fatale kept on moving and barged straight past Deadly De'Ath's second in command. Krool tried to stand her

23

ground, but it was all for nothing when I did much the same thing and knocked her off balance.

'We have to get out of here,' Fatale cried. 'The Crooked Council have decided to wash the sewers.'

'And?' shrugged Krool.

'And *that's* how they're washing them,' I said, pointing back along the tunnel. For a moment we all stopped and stared at what was coming up behind us. This was no river like Fatale had suggested.

No, this was more like a tidal wave.

'I think I would like to run now,' muttered Krool nervously.

So we did. Fatale was out in front, Krool was at the back, and I was somewhere in between.

'This way.' Fatale swerved to her left as the sewer turned a corner. Unfortunately for us, the water turned the corner too.

'Where are you going?' Krool called out.

'Anywhere that isn't here,' replied Fatale.

I followed her as she veered to her right. This went against everything I stood for. Not only was I putting my life in the hands of somebody else ... but that somebody else was Fatale De'Ath!

'I think there's a way out around here,' she said. Her torch light flashed over my eyes as she twirled on the spot. 'There are some steps that lead all the way up to the surface ... oh, my dress is getting wet!'

The water flowed over my flip-flops as I splashed my way towards her. 'Forget about your dress,' I yelled. 'It's not important.'

'Don't be like that, Stinky,' frowned Fatale. 'It's my favourite … even if it's not yours. I can tell you don't like it. It's not even in your top three.'

I shivered as the water rose up to my knees. 'Of course I don't like it,' I shot back at her. Then I checked myself. I knew Fatale well. How she thought. How she acted. How I should never get on her wrong side. 'I don't like it … because I love it,' I said hastily. 'It's my favourite too.'

'Really, Stinky?' grinned Fatale. 'Ah, that's the sweetest thing anyone's ever said to me. Right, we should probably think about getting out of this sewer before my dress gets ruined …'

I breathed a sigh of relief as Fatale spun away from me in search of the steps. Then I turned myself at the sound of a furious *splashing* behind me. It was Krool. Struggling to make her way through the ever increasing flow, she saw me looking and scowled. Charming. And I was just about to offer her a hand as well …

'I've found it, Stinky.'

I followed the voice and spotted Fatale over to my left, not far from where I was stood. She was wading towards a set of steps, identical to the ones I had used at the other end of the sewer.

'Give me a bunk-up,' she demanded.

The water was up to my waist now and rising. Just like us, it had nowhere to go.

Not yet, anyway.

I moved under Fatale and kept on pushing until she had made it all the way to the top.

'Do you think you can move the manhole cover?' I called up to her.

'Bit rude, Stinky,' replied Fatale, peering down at me. 'Just because I'm a girl it doesn't mean I'm weak. I'm perfectly capable of—'

'I know you are!' I blurted out. 'So just do it … now … please!'

Fatale rolled her eyes before placing both hands on the cover. It began to move. Not much. Only an inch or so, but I could still see a tiny chink of light coming from outside.

I took to the first step as the water washed over my shoulders. 'Try harder, Fatale,' I pleaded. 'You can do it. I know you can.'

'Yeah, *I* know I can.' To my despair, Fatale took her hands off the cover. 'There's just one thing I need to know before I do,' she said calmly. 'You're not really a sewer inspector, are you, Stinky?'

I stretched my neck as the water slapped against my chin. 'No,' I said honestly.

'I didn't think you were,' laughed Fatale. 'Good joke. I'll let you off this time, but if you ever try and trick me again …' With that, she pushed hard against the cover and then kept on pushing until it finally shifted to one side.

I could see daylight.

Fatale had already crawled out of the sewer by the time I set off after her. The water was right behind me, but it didn't matter.

Only one step to go …

'Not so fast!'

I felt a hand on my ankle. Before I knew it, I was tumbling down the steps until I landed with a *splash* and sank below the surface.

The first thing I saw when I lifted my head out of the water was Layla Krool. Not only was it her who had pulled me back, but now she had replaced me on the top step.

'Can weasel's breathe underwater?' With that, Krool climbed out of the sewer and began to slide the manhole cover back into place. 'I hope they can for your sake,' she said, grinning wickedly. 'If not for mine.'

5.'PERMISSION DENIED.'

Layla Krool had trapped me in the sewer.

Under the circumstances, the worst thing I could do was panic. And yet that was exactly what I did. Panic. With added *scare myself silly*. A hint of *completely lose the plot*. And a big dollop of *fall apart at the seams*.

But not for long.

Right, just stop and think about this for a moment. How well do you know me? A lot? A little? Or maybe not at all? Well, even if this is the first time we've ever met, there's one thing that all of us need to remember. It's one of life's many mysteries.

I, Hugo Dare, always get out of everything.

That's a fact.

Note to reader – contrary to what I just said, that is not a fact and you might want to cross your fingers at some point. And your toes. There. That should do the trick.

I ducked under the water and grabbed blindly for the steps. I found them at the third attempt and gripped on tight. Now it was a race. A race to see if I could hold my breath long enough to shift the manhole cover and get out of there.

It was a race I couldn't afford to lose.

Keep those fingers crossed …

I hurried up the steps the best I could until my head pressed against the cover. I knew that I would need both my hands so I wrapped my flip-flops under the next step up and tried to steady myself. The water was rocking me from side to side, but that was all. It could've been worse. And I knew it.

How long had I been holding my breath? Ten … eleven … twelve seconds …

I began to push. And the water pushed with me. Pressed up tight to the manhole cover, there was nowhere else for either of us to go. I twisted my toes as the flip-flops started to slip. If I fell away now there'd be no coming back.

How long had I been holding my breath? Sixteen … seventeen … eighteen seconds …

Time was running out. Summoning up every last ounce of strength, I pushed against the cover with all my might. It began to move. I was sure of it. Just not enough.

There was nothing more I could do. The water, however, refused to give in.

How long had I been holding my … whoa!

With a sudden *whoosh*, the manhole cover flew to one side as the water finally got its own way. The pressure had been released and there was nowhere else for it to go but up and out of the sewer.

As for me, I went the same way as the water. Up, up and away. Until …

When I landed it was with a wet *splat* on hard concrete.

I laid there for a moment, flat on my back, sucking in huge gulps of air.

You can uncross your fingers now. I'm okay. Well, *practically* okay. And that's about as good as things ever get so we might as well move on.

I couldn't lay there forever. Sitting up, I wiped the water out of my eyes so I could take in my surroundings. Unsurprisingly, Fatale and Krool were nowhere to be seen. A huge crowd, however, had gathered around me. They were increasing by the second, albeit at a distance for fear of getting soaked by the jet of water that continued to spray out of the sewer.

'Nothing to see here,' I said, clambering slowly to my feet. 'I'm a sewer inspector. I'm trained to deal with every possible sewer emergency you could ever imagine. Including this one. I'll be back soon. Once I've fetched a plug. A *big* plug.'

I put my head down and began to shuffle away before anybody asked me any awkward questions. Thankfully, the crowd parted to let me pass.

Where now? Home, I guess. If nothing else, I needed to take a shower and get dressed. Preferably in that order. The thought of it was enough to cheer me up a little. Okay, so it hadn't been the best of mornings, but there was no reason the afternoon had to go the same damp and dismal way.

A white Mini, however, seemed to suggest otherwise.

I watched as the car swung around the corner before skidding to a halt only inches from my flip-flops. Things didn't improve when the window dropped and a familiar face appeared in its place.

'Look at you, Hugo,' frowned Poppy. 'You're absolutely drenched.'

'Am I? I didn't realise,' I muttered through gritted teeth. 'Still, it's only a bit of water. It can't hurt me.'

Neither of those two sentences were correct. It wasn't only a *bit* of water and, back in the sewer, it almost did more than just hurt me.

'Take this,' said Poppy, throwing me a blanket. 'Warm yourself up.'

I wrapped it around my shoulders. Almost immediately, it seemed to take the edge off the chill.

'Our Deadly friend wasn't down there,' I said eventually. 'The sewer was a De'Ath-free zone.'

'Yes, we … um … know that already,' mumbled Poppy. 'There was a reported sighting of him just moments after you'd climbed down the steps. He was spotted coming out of a shop. He'd bought some marshmallows and an avocado. Everybody's got to eat I suppose. Even criminal masterminds.'

'Why didn't anybody come and tell me?' I groaned.

'We tried,' insisted Poppy, 'but none of us could fit through the manhole.'

I screwed up my face. 'So why flood the sewer then? You knew I was still down there.'

'That was the Big Cheese's idea,' Poppy shrugged. 'The eleven minutes were up. We had to get you out somehow. I've been driving around ever since trying to find you. And now I have. I hope you haven't made any plans because you're needed back at the SICK Bucket. Something's come up. Something big. A real emergency.'

'I need to get dressed first,' I sighed. 'I'll just nip home and—'

Poppy shook her head. 'Permission denied.'

'Really?' I tried again. 'Not even to take a—?'

'Permission denied,' repeated Poppy.

'Pops, look at me,' I moaned. 'I'm a mess. I've got to—'

'Permission denied,' said Poppy for a third time. 'Those were the Big Cheese's instructions. I'm sorry, Hugo, but this is urgent.'

'Fine.' I took a deep breath as I opened the door to the Mini. To my surprise, Poppy reached over and slammed it shut.

'Sorry, but a lift is out of the question,' she remarked.

'I thought we were in a hurry.' I pulled on the handle, but Poppy had locked the door. 'I thought I didn't have time to go home and get changed. I thought I had to get to the SICK Bucket as soon as possible. And that's why I thought you were going to give me a lift.'

'Yes, yes, yes and no way whatsoever!' said Poppy firmly. 'This Mini is my pride and joy. And you're wet, Hugo. Dripping from head to flip-flop. And – no offence intended – but you really stink. Who knew that the sewers smelled that bad? Listen, the best way we can do this is if you walk and I'll drive slowly beside you. It won't take long. Not if we get going now.'

I stared at her in stunned silence for at least eight-and-a-half seconds before I turned in the right direction and set off for the SICK Bucket. True to her word, Poppy drove slowly beside me.

'What were you doing?' she asked. 'In the sewer, I mean. Eleven minutes is a long time to be down there.'

'What was I doing?' I took a moment before I replied. Fatale De'Ath had arguably saved my life (even if Layla Krool had tried her best to ruin things). She was good like that. It also meant that I owed her. That was how these things worked.

'Yes, Hugo,' said Poppy, breaking my train of thought, 'what were you doing in the sewer?'

'Not much,' I said, refusing to look her in the eye as I stomped grumpily along the pavement. 'It was all a bit boring if I'm being honest.'

6.'OPEN YOUR EYES AND CONCENTRATE.'

We arrived at our destination exactly thirteen minutes after I had been blown out of the sewer.

Poppy was right; it wasn't a long journey. It would've been even shorter in the Mini, though. And warmer. And more comfortable. Not only that, but I would have avoided all the awkward stares as I wandered past, dripping from head to toe, in nothing but a pair of swimming trunks and a silk cravat.

Still, better to arrive wet than not at all (said no one ever).

Our destination was The Impossible Pizza. Yes, I know what you're thinking; Poppy said we were going to the SICK Bucket. And she was telling the truth. For those of you who don't know, the only way to get into SICK's secret underground headquarters is via the takeaway itself. I hope that makes sense. What's that? It doesn't? Not to worry. Just let the words pass over you and move quietly onto the next line. I promise not to tell anyone if you don't.

Poppy parked up on the roadside and met me by the door.

'You might want to prepare yourself, Hugo,' she warned me. 'Things are pretty weird inside.'

'Things are pretty weird outside as well,' I replied, glancing down at myself.

'No, this is serious,' Poppy insisted.

'In what way?' I shrugged. 'I've entered The Impossible Pizza so many times it's like clockwork. First, I creep in … then I tip-toe towards the counter … before Impossible Rita pounces—'

'This is different.' With that, Poppy twisted the knob three times to her left and twice to her right. The door opened and she walked inside. I was still none the wiser as I followed her.

That all changed, however, the moment I set foot on the premises.

Poppy was right. This was weird. Very weird. Weirder than I would ever have imagined.

Let me explain something to you. The Impossible Pizza may have looked like a takeaway from the outside, but looks can be deceptive. As far as food is concerned, you can neither eat in nor eat out. You can't even eat at all, in fact. And that's because it had never been open. Not once. No, the entire business was just a front. A cover for what lay deep in the bowels of the building.

And that's why the sight that greeted me when I first entered was like nothing I had ever seen.

The Impossible Pizza was bulging at the seams. Packed to the rafters. Absolutely chock-a-block. Quite simply, the takeaway was full. Full of people. Surely not customers, though.

'Told you it was weird,' whispered Poppy in my ear.

I tried to close the door, but found that a random leg, two arms and one enormous bottom were preventing me from doing so. That's how crammed it was in there. I took a deep breath and carefully maneuvered each body part out of the way before the door finally shut. Okay, so I couldn't move (and breathing wasn't that easy either), but I guess I could live with that.

'Over here, Hugo.'

Somewhat surprisingly, Poppy had found herself a tiny slice of space in one corner of the takeaway. I set off to join her without thinking. If I had, I would surely have realised that there was no way I could get there without treading on toes, knocking on knees, and generally barging into any other bodily bits that happened to get in my way. To my horror, my swimming trunks even fell down it was such a tight squeeze in there. Not that anybody noticed.

Oh, maybe one person did …

'Bad luck,' grinned Poppy, pretending to cover her eyes.

'Bad luck nothing,' I moaned. 'This is ridiculous.'

Using Poppy's shoulders to balance me, I climbed up onto the window ledge and began to count the heads. I gave up (definition – got bored) when I reached thirty-seven. There was at least double that number in there, though. Maybe triple. Men, women and children. From young to old, all shapes and sizes. I looked again and spotted Impossible Rita sat cross-legged on the counter. With her close-cropped hair, wild eyes and even wilder temper, she was SICK's first line of defence. I gave her a little wave and she scowled back at me. She wasn't that happy at the best of times – today she must have been positively furious.

'Since when did The Impossible Pizza open for business?' I wondered.

'Since never,' replied Poppy. 'These aren't customers. They're here to see the Big Cheese.' I stayed on the ledge, but crouched down so Poppy could speak a little quieter. 'I don't think you've realised yet, have you, Hugo?'

'I've realised that if anybody else dares to enter this takeaway the building will *pop* and we'll all end up on the other side of Crooked Elbow,' I remarked nervously.

Right on cue, the door jingled and another person squeezed into The Impossible Pizza.

'Brilliant,' I grumbled. 'Just what we didn't need—'

'You're still not seeing it, are you?' said Poppy. 'Open your eyes and concentrate.'

I did as she asked and picked out one customer (who wasn't really a customer) in particular. It was a small, stooped woman with a long scarf and even longer nose. What was Poppy seeing that I wasn't? Nothing seemed to stand out.

Unless …

My eyes rested on the woman's face. Her cheeks were wet. Wet with tears.

I shifted my gaze to the man beside her. He was so tall that his bald head brushed against the ceiling. His eyes, however, were damp as well. As were the small girl's beside him. And the flat-headed man in the opposite corner. And the boy in the baseball cap. And the man with the beard. No, that was a woman.

'Everybody's crying,' I murmured.

'Well spotted … eventually,' said Poppy.

'I know it's pretty squashed in here,' I began, 'but there's no need to get emotional about it.'

'That's not why they're crying,' insisted Poppy. 'I'll let the Big Cheese explain. Look over there. I think he's trying to get your attention even as we speak.'

I stood up straight and peered around the takeaway.

'Heads up, young Dare. Incoming arrival …'

I followed the Big Cheese's booming voice and spotted him by the rubbish chute. No, my mistake. Not *by* – he was *in* the rubbish chute. Sat inside to be precise. Half in, half out, he flicked his wrist and let go of something that flew across the takeaway. I lost it almost immediately.

It, however, had no trouble finding me as it hit me on the nose.

'Ouch!'

Moving quickly, I grabbed it out of the air before it had a chance to fall. I was surprised to find that it was a paper aeroplane. Stranger still, there was a message written on one of its wings.

SICK Bucket.
Now.
I said now!
Why are you still reading this?

I glanced over at the Big Cheese and gave him a thumbs up. That was the cue for him to let go of the sides and disappear backwards down the chute. Or so he thought. Unfortunately, he got stuck. Several grunts and the odd groan later, though, and he was back on the move.

'We've got to go,' I said, hopping down from the window ledge. 'The Big Cheese wants to see us in the SICK Bucket.'

'Better not keep him waiting then,' said Poppy, pushing her way through the assembled throng. 'Breathe in, Hugo. This might be even harder than it looks.'

7.'I WANT YOU TO DISAPPEAR.'

'Where have you two been?'

At the far end of the SICK Bucket there is a room called the Pantry. No, this isn't where we store our packed lunch. This is the Big Cheese's office. His *tiny* office.

And that was where we found him now, sat at his writing table with his head in his hands and a frown on his face.

'I've been waiting ages,' the Big Cheese grumbled.

'We got held up,' said Poppy, ushering me inside. She closed the door behind us, but then remained where she was (largely because there was nowhere else for her to go). 'Well, *one* of us got held up,' she said, correcting herself. 'And it wasn't me.'

'I was crawling between a woman's legs when she took offence and lifted me up by my ankles,' I explained. 'She only let go when she smelled my feet. Then she threw up all over the man beside her—'

'You've got an excuse for everything, young Dare,' the Big Cheese moaned. 'Admittedly, it is a little crowded in there. It's not my fault I'm so popular.'

'Popular, yes, but for all the wrong reasons,' said Poppy.

'They're only here because something really bad has happened.'

'It must be bad to make so many people cry,' I muttered. 'Don't tell me they've all just returned from the Crooked Onion Chopping Championship—'

'No, it's worse than that,' said Poppy, straight-faced. 'They've all lost their children.'

The Pantry fell silent. 'That's not funny,' I said, frowning.

'Perhaps not, but it's true,' insisted the Big Cheese. 'Everybody upstairs is either a mother or a father, a brother or a sister, an aunt or an uncle, a third cousin twice removed, or a—'

'Family member,' chipped-in Poppy.

'Exactly,' nodded the Big Cheese. 'The only thing they all have in common is that a child – *their* child – has gone missing.'

I screwed up my face. 'Kidnapped?'

'We don't think so,' said Poppy, shaking her head. 'There have been no ransom notes or demands. All we know for certain is that the children leave school but then never seem to make it home.'

'Have you arrested any teachers?' I asked. 'It's common knowledge they don't like kids. If you ask me—'

'We didn't,' said the Big Cheese gruffly.

'If you ask me,' I continued nevertheless, 'they'll have locked them all up in a store cupboard somewhere. Mr Shortcrust once did that to me. Ten minutes later I had eaten my way out. You can do anything when you're hungry—'

'Codswallop, young Dare!' bellowed the Big Cheese. He scowled at me for a moment before turning to Poppy. 'He *is* talking codswallop, isn't he, Miss Wildheart?'

'Do I really need to answer that, sir?' sighed Poppy. 'No, as far as we're aware the teachers are innocent. The children *are* somewhere, though, and we need to find out where.'

'You're right,' agreed the Big Cheese. 'Outer space was my first guess. This has got aliens written all over it.'

'No, it hasn't, sir,' argued Poppy. 'There has to be a more logical reason.'

'Ah, you mean magic,' the Big Cheese nodded. 'Abracadabra and all that nonsense. Or maybe they turned invisible. Or … oh, I can't believe I haven't thought of this before … maybe they all shrank in size. Really small like a pea. Watch where you tread, young Dare! Crush a child beneath your feet and their parents will go bananas!'

I decided to shift the conversation in a different direction before things got any stranger. 'So, how many children have actually gone missing, sir? Two? Three? Four?'

'Higher,' admitted the Big Cheese.

'Not six or seven?' I gasped. 'Eight? Nine?'

'Yes, nine,' said the Big Cheese. 'Nine … teen!'

'Nineteen?' I cried. 'That's terrible. Why have I never heard about this before?'

'We've managed to keep it under wraps,' replied Poppy. 'It's been a secret for a while now. No press. No news. No nothing. But that won't last forever. And that's why we have to act fast before any more children go missing.'

'You're not wrong,' I said. 'Nineteen is more than enough.'

'Yes, nineteen is a lot ... but I prefer twenty.' The Big Cheese stopped and winked at me. 'That's right, isn't it, young Dare? Twenty's a much better number, don't you think?'

'Tell me I'm wrong, sir,' I said slowly, 'but it sounds as if you want another kid to go missing.'

'That's because I do,' replied the Big Cheese matter-of-factly. 'And I want that child to be you!'

'Me?' I screwed up my face in horror. And then screwed it up some more when I realised the Big Cheese hadn't quite finished yet.

'I want you to disappear, young Dare,' he continued cheerfully. 'Vanish into thin air. Just like all those other poor children. Do you think you can do that for me?'

'Definitely,' I replied, resting my fingers on the door handle. 'I can walk straight out of the SICK Bucket this minute and you won't see me again for the rest of the day.'

'I don't think that's what he means,' said Poppy, before I had a chance to leave the Pantry.

'No, I know exactly what he means,' I moaned. 'And I'm not doing it!'

The Big Cheese slammed his hand down on the table in anger. 'You can't just say no, young Dare!' he roared. 'This is your job! This is what I pay you to do!'

'Erm ... no, it's not, sir,' I argued. 'I don't get paid. Not ever. I just do this for free. I thought everybody did.'

'Oh, this is awkward,' muttered the Big Cheese, glancing at Poppy. 'Young Dare seems to think that we're all as stupid as he is. I mean, that's not even possible, is it? I'd still be at least three times smarter than him even if I sliced off my own head and hid it under my armpit!'

'You do know I can hear you, don't you, sir?' I said.

'I do now,' the Big Cheese shrugged. 'Right … where were we? Ah, yes. Nothing personal, young Dare, but isn't it about time you disappeared?'

My shoulders slumped in despair. 'Why me, sir?'

'You're the only child agent we have,' explained the Big Cheese. 'And, besides, it's not as if we'll miss you whilst you're gone—'

'That's not helping, sir,' said Poppy hastily. 'The thing is, Hugo, I don't mean to be the bearer of bad news, but you really are the perfect spy for the mission at hand.'

'If you say so,' I sighed. 'Just don't tell me I have to do it with only my swimming trunks for company.'

'Of course not,' said Poppy. 'You won't be … *going missing* until tomorrow. Straight after school.' She paused. 'You are okay with this, aren't you, Hugo?'

I was about to say *no* when the Big Cheese answered for me.

'You bet he is!' he boomed. 'Young Dare is the hero that all those parents have been crying out for. That's why they're crying now. They're crying with joy because Young Dare is about to disappear and find their children.'

'I don't think that's why they're crying, sir,' I frowned.

'Maybe it is, maybe it isn't,' laughed the Big Cheese. 'Either way, you should think about heading home now and relaxing. Put your feet up and chill out. Say goodbye to your mum and dad because you might never see them again—'

'Sir!' A furious Poppy shook her head at the Big Cheese.

'I'll see you out, Hugo,' she said, placing a hand on my back. 'I'll even give you a lift home if you want. It's only fair under the circumstances. Is there anything else you need to know before we leave?'

'Just one thing.' I stood my ground in the Pantry until I caught the Big Cheese's eye. 'What if I don't come back, sir? What if I really do go missing … for good?'

The Chief of SICK held my stare before he eventually broke the silence. 'Then you'll have failed,' he said bluntly. 'And that's not going to happen now, is it, young Dare?'

8. 'WHO'S A PRECIOUS BABY?'

School was over for the day.

Worst luck.

Yes, I know what you're thinking. I should have been ecstatic, right? Jumping for joy. Hopping with happiness. But I wasn't. Instead, I was nervous. And on edge. And just a little bit grumpy. Hey, it's not my fault I'm in a bad mood. I'm sure *you* would feel the same way if somebody wanted you to disappear.

Shuffling slowly through the school gates, I waited until there was no one in sight before I removed a tiny ear piece from the pocket of my blazer. The Big Cheese had given it to me the previous day as I left the SICK Bucket. I switched it on and slotted it carefully inside my ear. It was a three way thing. Not only could I hear both the Big Cheese and Poppy, but both the Big Cheese and Poppy could hear me. We could communicate, in secret, like the spies we were.

Talking of which ...

'Can you hear me, young Dare?' That was the Big Cheese. As usual, his voice was loud enough to make my ears weep.

I moved hastily away from the Crooked Comp' and stepped into the shadow of a huge tree before I finally spoke. 'Yes, I can hear you, sir. Loud and clear.'

'Can you hear me?' asked the Big Cheese again. 'Can … you … hear … me?'

'Yes, I can hear you, sir,' I repeated. 'I've already told you that. But can *you* hear me?'

'Is there anybody there?' yelled the Big Cheese. I winced as the earpiece vibrated against my eardrum. 'Where is he, Miss Wildheart? I knew he'd mess this up. He can't be trusted to do anything. He's an absolute calamity. A complete disaster. My pet tortoise could do a better job than young Dare. And he passed away four years ago—'

'I'm here, sir,' I said, trying not to shout myself.

'He's useless,' continued the Big Cheese. 'Uselessly useless. Useless all year round. Even when he's asleep.'

'If I may, sir …' That was Poppy. 'It's not Hugo who's got the problem – it's you. You need to turn your volume up.'

The earpiece made a strange *buzzing* sound. 'Can you hear me now, young Dare?' the Big Cheese asked.

'Yes, sir,' I sighed.

'Splendid,' the Big Cheese boomed. 'And I can hear you, too. Problem solved.' There was an awkward silence. 'I don't suppose,' the Big Cheese began. 'No, you couldn't have … not possible … unless … you didn't happen to pick up anything I just said, did you?'

'Every word, sir,' I said honestly. 'I especially liked it when you compared me to your tortoise.'

'That was a joke,' the Big Cheese insisted. 'Morty the torty would've made a rubbish spy. And as for the rest of it … you must've misheard. Don't worry; I won't hold it against you. Right, when you've finished apologising, young Dare, you can crack on with the job at hand. The sooner you go missing the better. You have remembered to take the longest possible route home, haven't you?'

'I have now.' With that, I turned right instead of left and set off along the pavement. 'How long should this longest route actually be?'

'That depends,' replied the Big Cheese. 'Maybe you could just stay out until the aliens show up and take you away. Or you get sucked into some kind of black hole. Or the pavement opens up and you fall between the cracks.'

I stopped walking and looked down at my feet. 'Is that likely, sir?'

'Of course not,' said Poppy. 'We don't know what's going to happen, Hugo, but we'll be here when it does. We've got agents dotted around Crooked Elbow ready to spring into action the moment you give the word.'

'Thanks, Pops.' I was pleased to hear her voice. In all the madness, she was the one person who made everything seem even vaguely normal.

Unlike the Big Cheese. 'Maybe it'll be ghosts,' he remarked. 'Maybe they'll hide you under their sheets and whisk you away.'

'Ghosts don't wear sheets, sir,' muttered Poppy. 'People pretending to be ghosts wear sheets.'

'Same difference.' The Big Cheese snorted loudly to

mark the end of that particular conversation. 'Okay, young Dare, what are your co-ordinates?' he asked instead.

I screwed up my face. 'Pardon, sir.'

'Where are you?' explained Poppy. 'So we can track you.'

I turned a corner and read from the nearest road sign. 'I'm on Pete's Street.'

'I've got you,' said Poppy. I guessed she was following me on a map of Crooked Elbow. 'You're not far from Ali's Alley.'

'And only a stone's throw from Bridget's Bridge,' added the Big Cheese.

'Do you see anything peculiar yet?' asked Poppy.

I almost fell over as I peered at my own reflection in a shop window. 'Peculiar, yes ... but nothing unusual. It is starting to get cold, though. And dark. How long do you think I'll have to walk around for?'

'Not much longer,' answered Poppy.

'You hope,' cried the Big Cheese. 'This could go on for hours. What time do you normally go to bed, young Dare?'

I groaned out loud as I passed over Bridget's Bridge. It wasn't really a bridge as such – just a bump in the road. Which got me thinking. If I managed to rescue all these missing children then maybe they'd name something after me. Hugo's Highway certainly had a nice ring to it. Or Hugo's Hedge. Hugo's Hole. Hugo's Hump.

Yes. That was it. Hugo's Hump. Perfect.

Move over, Bridget. I'll take that bump in the road, thank you very much.

'Are you still there, young Dare?' hollered the Big Cheese.

I stopped daydreaming as I passed under Archie's Arch. 'Yes, sir. I'm here.'

'Young Dare,' barked the Big Cheese. 'Oh, where's he gone now?'

'Nowhere, sir. I'm here.' I came to a halt in the middle of the arch and fiddled with the earpiece. I could see two people coming towards me. A man and a woman. They were pushing the biggest pram I had ever seen. It was so big, in fact, that it almost filled the entire path.

'It's not you this time, sir,' said Poppy. 'Hugo's signal must have gone. I think we've lost him.'

Typical.

I stepped to one side and removed the earpiece from its resting place. Maybe Poppy was right. Maybe the signal had vanished the moment I stepped under the arch. I thought about turning back, but decided to wait until the couple with the pram had passed me by. I gave them a quick once over as they edged closer. The man was taller than any human I had ever set eyes on, with a face like concrete and a flat head of hair. His grey suit was at least three times too small for him and he appeared to be barefooted. In contrast, the woman was a fraction of his size in every way imaginable. Dressed in a long, black raincoat and a thin veil that covered much of her face, It was her that was pushing the pram.

I lowered my head as little and large drew level with me. At the same time something soft landed by my feet. It was a cuddly toy. I stared at it for a moment before the woman spoke and I snapped out of my trance.

'So sorry. Would you mind …?'

I crouched down and picked up the toy with the hand that wasn't holding the earpiece. The pram was right beside me when I stood up. Peeking inside, I expected to see a baby staring back at me.

How wrong could I be?

The sight that greeted me was so surprising that I had to turn away. Then I turned back again just to be certain.

Yes, I was right first time.

It wasn't a baby at all. Not even a really ugly baby.

It was a cat.

The toy fell from my fingers as the man stepped in front of me. We were so close now we were practically touching. I was about to say something when the woman reached around him and pressed something soft up to my face.

It was a handkerchief.

The second I realised what was happening was the same second that my whole world started to spin.

My body slumped and I was about to topple forward when the man grabbed me under the arms. The earpiece, however, wasn't so fortunate. I watched with blurry eyes as it slipped from my grasp and the man crushed it unknowingly beneath his feet. The next thing I knew I was being picked up and then lowered gently into the pram. The cat had even made room for me. I tried to sit up, but my body didn't seem to understand.

'Who's a precious baby?' cooed the woman, stroking my cheek.

Not me, that was for sure.

I wanted to scream and shout, but the only thing coming

DAVID CODD

out of my mouth was silence. My eyelids began to droop and I knew I couldn't fight it any longer. The last thing I saw was the woman as she lifted her hand and moved her veil to one side.

I could see her face.

And then ... nothing.

9. 'THIS IS AN EMERGENCY!'

I woke up.

Phew. Thank goodness for that. Because you never know, do you? That could have been it. The last page. The final chapter. The end of the book. As luck would have it, however, it's not. I'm still here. Alive and kicking. Well, alive at least. That's a start I suppose.

My eyes were open but I could barely see. That was due largely to a blinding light directly above me. I tried to lift my hands so I could block it out, but there were straps around my wrists preventing me from doing so. It didn't take me long to realise that the same straps were around my ankles.

Basically, I was strapped in. And, whichever way you look at it, that can never be a good thing.

I closed my eyes and tried to think. That was when the memories hit me. One after the other. Faster and faster and faster. Suddenly I could see myself in Archie's Arch ... little and large ... the pram ... the cuddly toy ... the cat ...

The handkerchief!

The memories ended abruptly. I had no idea how much time had passed since then, but it seemed like an absolute age.

Shifting my gaze away from the light, I tried again to check out my surroundings. As far as I could tell I was laid on a bed covered in a stiff, white sheet. The room was completely empty with white walls and no windows. Rolling my neck, I saw much the same thing on the other side of me. Oh, and a door. That was white, too. And closed.

So, where was I? A hospital most probably, but, if that was so, this was cleaner than any hospital I had ever known. Ridiculously clean, in fact. With an incredibly strong stench of disinfectant that violently attacked my nostrils whenever I dared to breathe.

Shock turned to anger as I strained against the straps. This was unacceptable. I wasn't a prisoner. And, besides, I had an itch. It was on the tip of my nose. And if I couldn't scratch it myself then someone else would have to scratch it for me.

'This is an emergency!' I called out. 'Please ... I need help!'

I pushed again, but the straps held firm as they pressed against my wrists. That hurt. And I didn't like it when it hurt. Not in the slightest.

I took a deep breath and was about to shout again when the door burst open.

'About time,' I grumbled.

I could hear footsteps edging closer to the bed before the light above me was finally moved to one side. To my surprise, there was a figure dressed in a white padded suit and face visor stood beside me. I couldn't be sure if it was a man or a woman. Or a doctor come to that. Or even an astronaut. Still, it would be rude not to call them something …

'If you don't mind, Doctor Astronaut, I've got an itch. Please be quick, though. It seems to be spreading …'

The figure in the padded suit ignored my demands as they set about inspecting me. First, they lifted my eyelids and shone a light straight into my eyes before poking me in both ears. I was about to complain when they switched their attention to my mouth. Something long and thin was stuck so far down my throat that I could feel it poking out of my belly button. To my relief, they didn't leave it there for long.

I was less relieved, however, when Doctor Astronaut swapped it for a sharpened pencil.

'What are you going to do with that?' I frowned, fearing the worst. The answer came when they took out a notepad and began to write. A few seconds later they put both back in their pocket.

'Is that it?' I asked. 'Examination over? Good. Now we can talk. What's going on? Because this isn't normal. Not even for me.'

Doctor Astronaut walked around the bed. They seemed to be heading towards the exit.

'Wait!' I shouted. 'Don't just leave me here. I need to know … what are you going to do to me?'

With that, Doctor Astronaut marched straight out of the room, stopping only to close the door behind them. I started to struggle. All of a sudden I had an urge to be free of the straps. Laid out like this I was useless. I couldn't do anything. Except wait. And I didn't like waiting. Especially when I had no idea what I was waiting for.

As luck would have it, though, I didn't have to wait for long.

A strange shuffling sound was enough to stop me mid-struggle. It was coming from the other side of the room but, when I looked, there was nothing there. Nothing except a metal grille in the top left-hand corner of the wall.

The shuffling stopped … but then the grille started to move. All of a sudden it was sliding back and forth. It was going to fall off …

And yet, somehow, it didn't. Yes, the grille had been completely removed from the wall, but now there were two hands holding it in mid-air.

'Nice to meet you, matey,' said a boy, sticking his head out of the opening. 'I was wondering when you were going to show up.'

10. 'YOU'RE A SURVIVOR.'

I watched in disbelief as a small boy in a blue boiler suit and white plimsolls crawled into the room.

'Let me just catch my breath,' he said, placing the grille gently on the ground. 'In … out … in … out. Yes, that'll do nicely. No need to shake it all about. It's one heck of a tight squeeze in that air vent, though. Good job I'm losing weight. Wouldn't want to get stuck halfway along now, would I?' The boy hesitated as he ran a hand over his severely shaven scalp. 'Oh, where are my manners?' he said, moving towards the bed. 'I'm number twelve, but you can call me Dodge. Everybody else does. Even my mum and dad.' An oddly vacant look passed over Dodge's face before he replaced it with a grin. 'What's your name?' he asked.

I answered without thinking. 'Pink Weasel.'

'Pink Weasel?' Dodge raised an eyebrow. 'Are you sure about that, matey?'

'No,' I said hastily. 'It's Hugo. I … erm … haven't got a number, though.'

'Not yet, but you will have,' muttered Dodge under his breath. He stuck out a hand for me to shake. I didn't, of course.

Not whilst my arms were still strapped to the bed. 'I'm guessing this might seem a little strange,' Dodge remarked.

'A little strange?' I screwed up my face. 'That's the understatement of the century. Please, Dodge, you need to tell me what's going on. Where am I for a start?'

'Keep your voice down, matey.' Tip-toeing across the room, Dodge put his ear to the door. 'We don't want him to hear us, do we?' he whispered.

'Who?' I asked.

'You'll find out soon enough,' frowned Dodge. 'I'm sorry, matey, but it's a long story and I haven't got the time. If I'm being honest I only came here to see where you fit in.'

'Fit in?' I said, confused.

'Everybody fits in somewhere,' explained Dodge. 'I mean, you're not about to burst into tears, are you?'

'Not that I'm aware of,' I replied.

'That's a start,' Dodge nodded. 'What about bullying? Is that your kind of thing? Picking on people? Making fun of them?'

'No,' I said quickly. 'Of course not.'

'This is getting better all the time,' grinned Dodge. 'One last thing. What are you like at school? You don't leave an apple on the teacher's desk, do you? Clean their shoes? Mow their lawns at the weekend?'

'I'm more of a teacher's pest than a teacher's pet,' I said honestly. 'Ask my old Headteacher if you don't believe me. No, on second thoughts, don't. Miss Stickler will probably rip your tonsils out of your ears if you dare to mention me—'

'Full house,' said Dodge, quietly clapping his hands

together. 'You're not a Sobber, or a Savage, or a Suck-up. Which means we're the same. You're a Survivor. Just like me. A normal, boring, run-of-the-mill Survivor. That's great news. Wait 'til the others find out.'

'What others?' I asked.

'I've got to go,' said Dodge, turning away from the bed. 'I've been here too long already. I'll see you later though, Hugo. I'm sure of it.'

'Dodge … wait.' I wanted to shout, but knew I couldn't. Instead, I watched as the small boy in the blue boiler suit picked up the metal grille and clambered silently into the air vent. A moment later the grille was back in place.

Resting my head on the pillow, I tried to make sense of what had just happened. Dodge had come and Dodge had gone, but I was still no closer to finding an answer to the one question that had bothered me from the moment I had first woken up.

Where was I?

I was all set to strain against the straps for the umpteenth time when a horrible *screeching* sound beat me to it. It was coming from a speaker in the corner of the room. I was still wondering what to make of it when the screeching stopped and a voice took its place.

'*Come, my child. I am ready for you. It is time that we were properly introduced.*'

I laid there completely still until the voice spoke again.

'*Exit the room and turn left along the corridor. Do not turn right. And do not keep me waiting.*'

I lifted my hands, surprised to find that the straps had

disappeared. Pushing the sheet away, I swung my legs over the side of the bed and planted both feet firmly on the ground. I wobbled for a moment before I found the strength to steady myself. I was shocked to see that I was dressed in the same blue boiler suit and white plimsolls as Dodge. Somebody had changed me out of my school uniform, but I had no recollection of it.

Confident that I wasn't about to fall, I crept forward until I reached the door. The handle dropped when I put my weight on it.

There was no turning back now.

One push later I found myself in the corridor. There were only two ways for me to go. Left and right? I thought about heading right, but then quickly dismissed it. The voice had warned me against it and, besides, this wasn't the time to be awkward. No, this was the time for answers. And the only way that was going to happen was if I did as I was told.

Turning to my left, I set off along the corridor. It was incredibly narrow with a thick, red carpet beneath my feet and closed doors on either side of me. It was only when I looked up that I saw another door in the distance.

Unlike the others, however, this one was wide open.

The closer I got, the more I could see. Like a toddler's bedroom turned up to the max, everything inside was either bright and colourful, or soft and fluffy. Or, worse still, both.

I came to a sudden halt when I reached the doorway.

'Enter,' said a voice from inside. 'I won't bite. I promise.'

11. 'ODD BY NAME, ODD BY NATURE.'

'Come closer, my child. Nobody likes a shy boy.'

The voice that spoke was the same one I had heard over the speaker. Peering around, I finally spotted a man lurking behind a bed in one corner of the room. He was dressed in an orange roll-neck sweater, stiff brown trousers, white socks and open-toed sandals. His sandy-coloured hair was brushed forward into a floppy fringe, whilst his nose was stuck up like an excited piglet and his mouth was set in a gap-toothed grin. I guessed he was about the same age as the Big Cheese, but much smaller in height and nowhere near as wide.

I took another step forward.

'That's better,' said the man, shuffling out from behind the bed. 'I can see you now. You're everything I remembered and more. A perfect addition to our wonderful little family.' The man swept his hair out of his eyes. 'Let me introduce myself. My name is Ebenezer Odd—'

'Odd by name, odd by nature,' I muttered under my breath.

'Oh, that's funny,' Odd giggled. 'I'll have to keep an eye on you, won't I? I thought that back in the examination room. Nobody's ever called me Doctor Astronaut before.'

I looked him up and down. 'That was you?'

'Naturally,' nodded Odd. 'I like to examine all my children when they first arrive. And you passed. Congratulations. That means you can stay. First, however, I need to take your details. Nothing too difficult. Height … weight … eating requirements—'

'Stop!' I lifted my hand without warning, causing Odd to step back behind the bed.

'No sudden movements please,' he said timidly. 'Or raised voices. I have a particularly nervous disposition. I'm easily frightened.'

I lowered my hand and started again. 'I wasn't trying to frighten you. It's just … no offence … but I don't want to stay. I'd rather be somewhere else.'

'There is no *somewhere else*,' remarked Odd curiously. 'Only here. With me. And Norman. And Mrs Snuggleflops. And all my other children. Why don't you take a seat and I can explain—?'

'No, let *me* explain.' I spoke firmly, but somehow managed to stop myself from shouting. 'I'm not staying here. That's a fact. And that's why I'm going to leave. You can try and stop me if you like—'

'I'd rather not,' said Odd swiftly. 'I would never try and prevent anyone from leaving. I'm far too delicate for anything like that.'

I hesitated for a moment before marching straight out of

Odd's bedroom. With nothing or no one standing in my way, I hurried back along the corridor as fast as I could. It didn't take me long to pass the door to the examination room. Odd had warned me not to come this way, but so what? Why should I listen to him?

I began to slow down. The corridor had come to an end, but there was another door. I yanked on the handle, but it held firm. Frustrated, I pushed against it with my shoulder, but it made no difference. That didn't stop me from trying again, though. And again. And again. And ...

Sweat was streaming down my face by the time I turned around and headed back the way I had just come. I tried every door I passed, but all of them were locked.

All except one.

And that was the door to Ebenezer Odd's bedroom.

'The wanderer returns,' smiled Odd, welcoming me back with open arms. 'That was rather embarrassing, wasn't it? Storming off like that? How humiliating! Such a silly ... little ... boy!'

I don't know what came over me because, next thing I knew, I was racing across the carpet with my fists clenched. I was aiming for Odd, and I had almost reached him when a sharp stinging pain hit me in the chest, stopping me dead in my tracks. It was so intense that my entire body spasmed and I fell to the ground in a sorry heap.

Then, as quickly as it had arrived, the pain vanished.

'Apologies,' said Odd, leaning over me. 'I told you I was very nervous.'

I sat up, struggling to catch my breath. 'What was that?'

'A shock to the system.' Odd held up a long, three-pronged stick by way of an explanation. 'An *electric* shock,' he revealed. 'My child zapper won't actually kill you; it's just a reminder. A reminder of what will happen if you ever try to hurt me again.'

'I wasn't going to hurt you,' I lied. 'I was just confused. I don't know what's going on.'

'Oh, you poor thing,' said Odd, patting me on the head. 'I know this must be difficult for you, but it really is for the best. Why don't you make yourself comfortable and I'll try to fill in the blanks?'

I picked myself up off the carpet and collapsed into a huge, padded chair beside me. It was even softer than it looked and instantly swallowed me up.

'That's *my* special seat, naughty,' said Odd, wagging a finger at me. 'Only I sit there. You can sit on the floor.'

I muttered something under my breath as I slipped off the chair.

'This is nice, isn't it?' said Odd, taking my place. 'I love story time, don't you?'

'Not particularly,' I replied.

'Good,' said Odd, ignoring me completely. 'Right, shall I begin? Once upon a time there was a sweet, sweet boy who came down from the ...' Odd stopped suddenly. 'What's wrong? Your face ... it's all scrunched up ... like an angry peanut. Don't you like my story?'

'I'm not a baby,' I grumbled. 'So stop treating me like one and answer my questions. Who are you?'

Odd gently shook his head. 'I've told you already. My

name is Ebenezer Odd … but you can call me Daddy.'

'Daddy?' I blurted out. 'That's not going to happen.'

'That's what all my children say when they first arrive,' said Odd, chuckling to himself. 'They soon change their minds, though. I can be very persuasive. Maybe another shock to the system will—'

'Not be necessary,' I chipped-in. 'Just tell me. Where are we?'

'We're in the loveliest place known to mankind,' purred Odd. 'A safe haven. A solitary sanctuary. A thing of beauty away from the horrors and vulgarity of everyday life.'

'You've just described my shedroom,' I sighed. 'So, where is this lovely, safe, solitary, thing of beauty exactly?'

'You're teasing me,' frowned Odd. 'Maybe you're right, though. Maybe it is time I put you out of your misery.' The frown turned to a smile as he leapt to his feet. 'This is Odd Island,' he announced, spinning on the spot with his arms outstretched. 'Welcome to the rest of your life.'

12.'MY ISLAND, MY RULES.'

Odd Island.

Where?

That was the first thought that crossed my mind. I had never heard of it and had certainly never been there. As far as I was aware it wasn't on any map of Crooked Elbow and its surrounding area. And yet here I was. On an island that didn't even exist.

'It's a lot to take in,' Ebenezer Odd admitted. 'I know that. Don't let it fluster you, though. Maybe things will feel a little more ... *real* once I've shown you to your living quarters. This way, Twenty ...'

I stayed seated. 'Twenty?'

'That is your number,' explained Odd. 'All my children have a number. Your names are no longer necessary. They are nothing but an echo of your past.'

With that, Odd scuttled out of the bedroom. He had barely left me to it when I scrambled to my feet and hurried after him.

'Not too close,' he warned me. 'I'd hate for you to get another nasty shock.'

'You're not the only one.' I backed away and then pointed along the corridor, careful not to touch Odd by accident. 'All the doors are locked,' I said.

'Not to me they're not,' replied Odd smugly. 'My island, my rules. That's the way things are around here. You'll get used to it, I'm sure. You'll have to. You don't have a choice.'

Odd stopped at the door I had struggled to shoulder barge and removed something small from his pocket. With a flick of his wrist, he waved it in front of a panel just above the handle and the door began to open. He stepped out first. I followed and …

Wow!

I moved quickly to cover my eyes. It was so bright that I started to wonder how long I had been asleep for. A day? A week? Surely not an entire month? As far as I could remember we had been stuck in the drabbest depths of winter when I had left school on that fateful Monday. This, however, was more like the height of summer. Not only was it blindingly bright out there, but any chill in the air had vanished and not even the slightest trace of a breeze remained.

I squinted through my fingers and realised that it wasn't the sun that was shining down on me, but a number of tall spotlights. I counted four in total before I had to look away. Each of them was at the top of a wooden tower and as powerful as anything you'd find at a sports stadium. What I couldn't quite figure out, though, was why they were on full beam in the middle of the day?

'Don't look at the lights,' advised Odd.

'Too late,' I grumbled. 'You could've told me that ten seconds ago.'

'That's the Nerve Centre,' said Odd, pointing behind me at the building we had just exited. An extremely long, single-storey construction, it had no windows and a flatter than flat roof. 'And this is the courtyard,' continued Odd, gesturing around at the wide open space that surrounded us. 'You will work here … exercise here … you may even eat here from time to time. What you will not do, however, is try and escape from here. There is an electric fence running all the way around the perimeter of the compound. It's for your own safety, of course. We're not trying to keep you in – we're trying to keep them out!'

I screwed up my face. 'Them?'

'Wild wolves,' explained Odd. 'We have a problem with them on Odd Island. Their numbers have increased dramatically over the years. We rarely see them – they tend to hide in the fog that covers much of the island – but we can always hear them. They howl when they're hungry. And they're *always* hungry. Don't look so nervous; the fence will keep them out. And even if they did somehow manage to sneak in, the guards would soon make sure that they got no further.'

'You have guards?' My eyes shifted in every direction. 'I can't see them.'

'That's the way I like it,' smiled Odd. He lifted a finger and pointed up at the lights. 'Try not to stare, but there's a guard positioned on each of the watchtowers.'

I shielded my eyes from the glare as I looked up. Odd

was right; there was an outline of a human body stood under the spotlights. I couldn't make out if it was a man or a woman, but they were clearly armed.

'I don't think I have to tell you what will happen if you try and escape,' began Odd, wagging a finger at me. 'If the fence doesn't stop you, the guards will. And if the guards don't, the wolves will. And if the wolves don't, well, the island itself will hold you tight and refuse to let go. You are still listening, aren't you, Twenty?'

'Of course,' I replied. That wasn't true. Not only was Odd walking and talking to himself, but he had also edged ahead of me. It was enough to get me thinking ...

If Odd couldn't see me then he probably wouldn't miss me if I went exploring.

I realised what a bad idea that was when I turned sharply and crashed face-first into something uncomfortably solid.

It was a man. A big man. Bigger than big with enormous shoulders and a huge chest. His face was set like concrete, his hair was flat to his head, and his eyes stared blankly into space. Like me, he was dressed in a boiler suit, although his was white in colour and at least three sizes too small for him. He was also barefooted.

My mind cranked into gear and a memory stirred. I had seen this man before. Under Archie's Arch with the pram. But that meant ...

'Oh look who it is,' cried an excited Odd, as he finally turned around. 'Say hello, Norman.'

The big man slowly opened his mouth. 'Hello ... Norman.'

'Yes, that's close enough,' sighed Odd. 'I have lots of children, but Norman's one of a kind. He's my special boy. I was hoping that you two would cross paths before long—'

'We've already met,' I blurted out. 'But then you would know that, wouldn't you? Because you were there. It was you who pressed the handkerchief to my face. You drugged me.'

'I don't know what you mean,' smirked Odd. 'And neither does Norman. We're both very private people. We go everywhere together, but never travel far. As you can probably tell, Norman is a man of very few actions and even fewer words. He chooses not to speak and I choose not to force him. I know I don't look old enough, but I've cared for him all his life. Even from a baby, I knew he'd be big and strong. And I was right. Time has passed and now it's Norman's turn to take care of me. He doesn't like anybody being rude or hurting my feelings. It makes him mad. Do you understand what I'm saying, Twenty? You wouldn't want to see Norman mad now, would you?'

'I wouldn't want to see Norman *at all*,' I remarked. 'And, at a guess, he feels much the same way about me. He's not looked down once. Does he even know I'm here?'

With Odd's special boy still gazing into the distance, I lifted a hand, ready to click my fingers in his face so I could get his attention. Despite his size, Norman moved surprisingly quickly and swatted my hand away. Next thing I knew he had clenched his fist and brought it crashing down on my head. I closed my eyes and tried not to fall over as the pain washed over me. Now that hurt. I hadn't seen the fist coming, and nor had I expected it.

Next time, however, I would be ready.

'Now, now, Norman, be kind to our new arrival,' said Odd, frowning at his huge companion. 'It's not Twenty's fault he doesn't understand our little ways.'

'Little ... ways,' grunted Norman.

'Shall we continue?' said Odd, setting off across the courtyard. 'Preferably before you try and run off again ...'

I could feel Norman pressing against me so I started to walk. We were heading towards a row of large wooden huts in the distance. Like the Nerve Centre, they all had a flat roof and no windows.

'You will be sharing a dormitory with four other children,' revealed Odd, stopping at the first hut we came to. 'This is exciting, isn't it, Twenty?'

'That's one way to describe it,' I muttered.

Odd skipped up a steep metal ramp and pushed open the door. 'Let me introduce you to your new family,' he said, ushering me inside. 'I'm sure you'll all get along fabulously.'

13.'YOU ARE A CATERPILLAR!'

The door to the hut closed behind us.

Things had seemed so much bigger from the outside. Yes, there were no windows to let in any light, but I guessed it had more to do with the fact that five single beds, a small table with two chairs, and a sink and a bucket had all been squeezed inside. Someone from a different time may even have said there was barely room to swing a cat in there (but seeing as cat swinging is no longer permitted anywhere on the planet then I don't think I'll bother).

There was, however, still room for four children amongst all the furniture. Two boys and two girls. Both girls had been seated around the table, before choosing to stand when we had entered, whilst one of the boys was perched on the edge of the nearest bed to me. There was a pair of crutches beside him. A perfectly good weapon if and when I needed.

The final boy, meanwhile, was leaning against one of the walls, trying desperately not to smile.

It was Dodge. The first person I had spoken to on Odd Island (as well as the only person I had ever known to climb in and out of an air vent).

I avoided eye contact and remained completely straight-faced, determined not to give anything away. For all Odd knew, this was the first time any of us had ever met. And, for Dodge's sake if nothing else, that's the way it had to stay.

'Hello, my children,' said Odd cheerfully.

'Hello, Daddy,' the four replied in harmony. I tried not to show it, but that surprised me.

'This is the day we've all been waiting for,' began Odd. I backed away as he tried to grab my elbow, but didn't get far before Norman pushed me forward again. 'We have a new arrival,' announced Odd, holding my arm aloft. 'The final piece of the jigsaw. A wonderful addition to our already perfect little family. As from today he will be joining you here, in your dormitory, and I urge you all to make him feel as comfortable as possible. His name is Twenty—'

'No, it isn't,' I butted-in. 'I'm not a numb ... ow!'

I dropped to my knees as a sudden surge of electric passed up and down my body.

'That's your second warning,' scowled Odd, hovering over me with the child zapper. 'You're being awfully difficult, Twenty. I hope these shocks to the system don't have to become too regular an occurrence.'

'No,' I said hastily. 'Definitely not.'

'Definitely not ... *Daddy*,' frowned Odd. 'If you're so keen to interrupt me all the time then maybe you'd prefer to introduce yourself rather than have me do it.' Odd paused. 'Go on. We're all waiting.'

I gritted my teeth as I clambered unsteadily to my feet. No, I didn't prefer it. Not in the slightest. Now, however, wasn't the time to argue. 'My name is Twenty,' I said sullenly. 'Nice to meet you all.'

'Well done,' chirped Odd, clapping his hands together. 'That wasn't so hard now, was it? As for the others, this is Twelve,' he said, gesturing towards Dodge. 'Like you, he used to be a little … demanding at times. Quite troublesome, in fact. Then he saw the error of his ways and turned his life around. Now he's absolutely adorable. An excellent example of what I'm trying to achieve here—' Odd stopped suddenly. 'Stand up straight when I'm talking about you, Twelve.'

Dodge pushed himself off the wall without missing a beat. 'Sorry, Daddy.'

'That's more like it,' smiled Odd. With that, he switched his attention towards the boy on the bed. He had tight, curly hair, red cheeks and a round face. 'This is Thirteen,' said Odd. 'Poor, pitiful Thirteen. Oh, I can feel myself welling up already. His is such a sad, sad story—'

'It's no big deal,' said Thirteen, reaching for the crutches.

'It's no big deal … *Daddy*,' said Odd, correcting him. 'You are different, though. Compared to all your other brothers and sisters.'

'I can't feel my legs if that's what you mean,' Thirteen shrugged. 'It's all I've ever known, so I wouldn't—'

'I can't feel my legs if that's what you mean … *Daddy*,' stressed Odd. 'You know how much it upsets me when you forget to call me that. Still, if there's anyone I'm prepared to forgive it's you, my brave, brave boy. My super-duper soldier.'

'Thanks, Daddy,' sighed Thirteen. 'That means a lot, Daddy. From you of all people, Daddy. Over and out, Daddy.'

I bit down on my lip to stop myself from smiling. Odd may have been none the wiser, but Thirteen was almost certainly mocking him.

'Just the two to go,' said Odd, waving a hand at the girls stood beside the table. 'Nine could teach you a lot about respect, Twenty. She's the strong, silent type. Very mature for her age. Eighteen, meanwhile, hasn't quite come out of herself yet, but there's still time. If anything, she's like a caterpillar. If she tries hard enough she might just become a butterfly. Do you agree?'

'Yes, Daddy,' replied Nine gruffly. I figured she was about a year or two older than me. Fifteen at most, but probably fourteen. She had a stern face for someone so young, a square, solid jaw, and small eyes that refused to fully open. Broad shoulders and big arms filled her boiler suit. The strangest thing about her, though, was her bowl-shaped haircut. If anything it reminded me of a hairy mushroom. Not that I'd ever dare to tell her that.

'Thank you, Nine, but I wasn't talking to you,' said Odd. 'I was talking to Eighteen. Are you or are you not a caterpillar?'

Nine nudged the girl beside her so hard that she almost fell over. I wasn't surprised. Eighteen looked so weak she could barely brush the hair out of her face, let alone stand up.

'Can you hear me?' hollered Odd. 'You are a caterpillar!'

Eighteen's mouth fell open. She was trying to speak, but nothing was coming out.

'That is not an adequate enough answer,' spat Odd. 'Go and shake some life into her please, my special boy. Nothing too painful. You know how much I dislike violence …'

Norman was on the move before Odd had even finished speaking. Eighteen finally blew her hair away and I caught sight of her face for the very first time. Her eyes were wet and her bottom lip was wobbling. She was absolutely petrified. And that was why I decided to act.

Snatching one of the crutches out of Thirteen's hands, I crouched down and dangled it in front of Norman's feet as he marched past. It wasn't enough to trip him up, but it did knock him off his stride as he stumbled forward.

'You,' he grunted, turning to confront me.

'Me?' I dropped the crutch back on the bed and held up my hands. 'I don't know what you mean.'

'What happened?' wondered Odd, confused. 'I didn't see.'

'No, me neither,' I said innocently. 'I had my eyes closed … accidents do happen, though …whoa!'

Without warning, Norman lifted me off the ground and slammed me against the wall.

'You,' he repeated. 'You … make… me … fall.'

'Not deliberately,' I said, struggling to breathe. 'I'm just clumsy.'

I gasped as Norman pushed a little harder.

'You're hurting him,' said Dodge, rushing towards us.

'Back away, Twelve,' warned Odd, lifting the child

zapper. 'This is not your place to interfere.' He waited until Dodge had done as he asked before he spoke again. 'That's quite enough thank you, my special boy,' he said softly. 'I'd hate for you to go *too* far … again. It was bad enough the first time … even worse the second time … and let's not mention the third time …'

Norman dropped me on command and I landed with a *thud*.

'Maybe we should leave them to it,' suggested Odd, turning towards the door. 'Tensions are running a little high and I'd hate for Twenty to get the wrong impression. Odd Island is not a place of conflict; it is a place of peace.' Odd hesitated. 'One last thing,' he said, glancing over his shoulder. 'What are you, Eighteen?'

'She's a caterpillar, Daddy,' replied Nine, answering for her.

'That's right,' nodded Odd. 'That's exactly what she is. But now I want Eighteen to say it herself. What … are … you?'

'She can't do that, Daddy,' blurted out Thirteen.

'Speak when you're spoken to!' Odd shot back. 'Now, Eighteen, what are you? Say it. Say it clearly. Say it so everyone can hear.'

Eighteen closed her eyes. 'I'm a c-c-caterpillar,' she stuttered.

'That's right,' cried Odd. 'You're a caterpillar. A small, shrivelled-up caterpillar. A small, shrivelled-up caterpillar who'll never be a butterfly. Not ever. No, you're more like a moth. And who likes moths? Nobody, that's who.' Odd stopped to draw a breath. 'Very good, my children. I think I've finished here.'

With that, Ebenezer Odd left the hut. Norman, as I'd already come to expect, followed without another word.

I waited for the door to close behind them,

'That was ... interesting,' I said, screwing up my face. 'Now, does anybody want to tell me what on earth we're all doing here?'

14.'WHAT IF WE NEVER GET THROUGH THIS?'

Dodge skipped across the hut and pressed a finger to my lips.

'Wait,' he whispered.

At the same time, Nine picked up the bucket and wandered over to the furthest corner. There was something down there on the floor. Something so small that you could easily miss it. I watched as Nine turned the bucket upside down, placing it gently over the object. Then she sat on it.

'That's better,' said Dodge, removing his finger. 'We're safe to speak now. Odd can't hear us.'

'What's under the bucket?' I asked.

'A bug,' Dodge revealed. 'Some kind of listening device hidden inside an air freshener. Odd likes to hear what we have to say.'

'And now he can't,' I said, impressed.

'Exactly,' nodded Dodge. 'We can say what we like. Starting with this ...' Dodge put an arm around my shoulder. 'I knew you'd end up in here, Hugo. You're no Sobber or Suck-up or Savage. I could tell that just by looking at you. You're like me. You're a Survivor. We're the perfect fit—'

'Oh, this is nice,' smirked Thirteen. 'I didn't know you two were the best of buddies.'

'Not jealous, are you?' laughed Dodge. 'Still, at least Odd likes you. You are his brave, brave boy, after all. His super-duper soldier.'

'Yeah, lucky me,' moaned Thirteen. At the same time, he grabbed his crutches and pushed himself up off the bed. 'The name's Will, but everyone calls me Wheelie,' he said, holding up his hand.

I gave him a high-five. 'Wheelie?'

'Because of my wheelchair,' said Wheelie. 'Bit obvious really. Still, anything has got to be better than Willy No Legs.'

'But then that wouldn't be true, would it?' remarked the girl called Nine. 'You have got legs. They just don't work very well.'

'Thanks for reminding me,' muttered Wheelie. 'If it wasn't for you I might never have realised.'

'And if it wasn't for you I might sleep better at night,' grumbled Nine. 'Your snoring is so loud it makes the walls shake. It got so bad one night I thought the ceiling was going to collapse. That's Angel by the way,' said Nine, pointing over at Eighteen. 'She doesn't say much, but I'm guessing you've figured that out for yourself. And I'm Mo.'

'Also known as Maureen,' added Wheelie.

'No, just Mo,' insisted Mo sternly. 'I don't like Maureen.'

'Don't be so harsh on yourself,' grinned Wheelie. '*I* like you, Maureen. Do you like me?'

'Call me Maureen again and there won't be much of *you* left to like,' replied Mo, smashing her fist into her palm.

'You'd better get used to this because it never stops,' sighed Dodge. 'These two are always digging at each other. It's nothing serious, though. They're good friends really. Even if they have only known each other since they first got here.'

'And where is *here* exactly?' I asked. 'I know we're on Odd Island – I just don't know where Odd Island is.'

'Nobody does,' said Wheelie, shaking his head. 'None of us have ever heard of it before. It's almost as if it doesn't exist.'

'Which probably explains why we're still here,' shrugged Dodge. 'How can we be rescued if the police, or the army, or whoever, haven't found the island yet? They will do, though. I'm sure of it.'

'Yeah, me too,' I said. And I had. Found the island, I mean. At that very moment, there was nothing I wanted more than to tell the others who I really was and why I was there.

I wanted to … but I didn't.

How could I? If they knew I was a spy, they would think I was there to rescue them. Yes, that was the plan. Eventually. First, however, I had to figure out how to do it.

'What's wrong, matey?' asked Dodge, poking me in the ribs. 'You look confused.'

'No, not confused,' I replied. 'I'm just … surprised. You all seem so relaxed. Laughing … joking … messing about.

And yet … all of you have been kidnapped, right? Snatched off the streets? You must be missing your families …'

With that, Angel burst into tears.

I screwed up my face. 'Whoops. Was it something I said?'

'No, not something – *everything!*' remarked Wheelie, rolling his eyes at me. 'Don't let it worry you, though. We all put our foot in it from time to time.'

'Angel's just a little emotional at the moment,' said Dodge, wandering across the hut so he could put an arm around her shoulder. 'This place can get to you once in a while, but you have to stay strong. It's the only way that any of us can get through this.'

'The thing is, what if we never get through this?' muttered Mo. 'What if we have to stay here forever?'

Dodge moved quickly to cover Angel's ears. 'That's not going to happen,' he said.

'You don't know that,' argued Wheelie.

'No … but I do.' All eyes turned towards me when I spoke. 'We won't be here forever. We might not even be here next Thursday. You have to believe me.'

'Don't make promises you can't keep,' said Mo firmly.

'Then I won't,' I replied. 'But Dodge is right. We have to stay strong. Odd can't tell us what to do and he certainly can't keep us here against our will. And that big goon Norman can't push us around whenever he wants either. And that's why if … no, *when* we get the chance, we'll try and escape. That's not a promise; it's a fact.'

'Nobody's ever escaped from Odd Island before,' declared Mo.

'Perhaps,' I shrugged, 'but then nobody's ever eaten their own weight in jelly babies either, but that doesn't mean I'm not prepared to give it a go.'

'Fair enough,' Wheelie laughed. 'You've convinced me. Anyone would think you're some kind of super hero the way you're talking.'

Oh. Slightly awkward. 'No, not a super hero,' I said hastily. 'Let me think … I'm a—'

I was stopped mid-sentence by the sound of a ringing bell. Coming from a speaker in the top corner of the hut, it was loud enough to drown me out before I said something I would almost certainly regret.

'What's that?' I wondered.

'Lunchtime,' groaned Wheelie.

'You make it sound like a bad thing,' I said, rubbing my stomach eagerly.

'Wait and see,' laughed Dodge, as he made his way towards the exit. 'Just don't get your hopes up, okay?'

15.'I'M NOT EATING THAT!'

Dodge opened the door and we stepped outside.

I avoided the glare of the searchlights and kept my head down as I looked out over the courtyard. The first thing I saw was a group of children sat cross-legged on the ground. Dressed identically to me, they had formed a circle and were now facing inwards.

Stood in the middle of them, on a pink fluffy rug, was Ebenezer Odd.

He wasn't alone. The cat I had seen in the pram under Archie's Arch was there, too. Odd was trying to cradle it like a baby, but the cat's response was to squirm like mad before it eventually wriggled free of his grasp.

'There, there, Mrs Snuggleflops,' said Odd, stroking the cat before it scampered off. Looking up, he saw us coming. 'Don't dilly-dally, my children,' he snapped. 'Lunch is about to be served and I'd hate for you to miss it.'

'I wouldn't,' muttered Dodge under his breath. 'I'd be quite happy to go without.'

I followed him as he joined the circle. Okay, so the ground wasn't as cold as I'd imagined, but it was still much harder than I would have hoped. I shuffled about and tried to get comfortable, but it made no difference. My bum still hurt whatever I did.

In an effort to distract myself from the pain I cast a spy-like eye over the faces that surrounded me. A mixture of boys and girls, the children were all roughly the same age as me, give or take a year or two. Even at first glance it wasn't difficult to make out the four different groups that Dodge had spoken about. To my left, three boys and two girls were huddled together with their heads down, snuffling and sniffing as they wiped their faces on their sleeves. I guessed that these were the Sobbers. To my right, four girls and a boy were staring up at Odd in wonder, hanging on his every word whilst eager to catch his eye whenever the chance arose. They had to be the Suck-ups.

The final group, meanwhile, were straight ahead of me. Three boys and two girls, they were all sat with their arms crossed as they glared over in my direction. The biggest of them – a huge brute of a boy with spiky hair and chubby cheeks – even mimed running a finger across his throat. Charming.

These were the Savages. At least, I hoped they were. Otherwise I was in trouble.

'Two down, three to go,' sighed Odd.

I glanced over my shoulder and saw that Wheelie, Mo and Angel were still yet to join us. Stood at the top of the ramp, the two girls were assisting Wheelie as he climbed into his wheelchair. It looked like a well-rehearsed manoeuvre, but I still shifted on to my feet, ready to go and help. Dodge moved quickly and placed a hand on my leg. He shook his head, the message loud and clear.

Don't.

And, for once, I didn't.

'In your own time,' moaned Odd, as the three of them made their way towards the circle. I shuffled to one side so Wheelie could squeeze in beside me, whilst Mo and Angel sat on the other side of him.

'Have you finished? Thank goodness for that,' Odd muttered. He clapped his hands to get everyone's attention. 'Are you feeling hungry, my children?' he asked. There was the faintest of murmurs from somewhere within the circle. 'Of course you are. Come, come, Norman, the children are waiting patiently ...'

Right on cue, Norman emerged from the Nerve Centre. He was pushing a trolley, it's wheels rattling as they bounced up and down on the bumpy ground. Fearful for their safety, the children nearest to him scrambled to one side so he could enter the circle.

'Phew, that smells ... unusual,' remarked Odd, backing away from an enormous cooking pot in the middle of the trolley. 'Don't tell me what it is. I'd rather not know. Right, let's not keep them waiting, my special boy ...'

With that, Norman set off around the circle, handing out a bowl and spoon to each child he passed. I waited for my turn, but then refused to take them nicely. Norman didn't appear to care and dropped both without breaking stride. The bowl bounced up off the ground, whilst the spoon hit me on the head. Yes, you don't have to tell me that was my own fault. I'm not stupid. Not much, anyway.

I picked them up and wiped them clean on my boiler suit. They were made of plastic with no sharp edges, almost like something a toddler would use. I was still studying them, in fact, when Norman began his second lap of the circle. This time he was carrying the pot. It was so heavy he had to hold it with both hands. Stumbling to a halt at each child, he blindly poured its contents into every bowl he came to. Try as he might, he was unable to prevent it from dribbling down his fingers onto his boiler suit.

I waited until Norman had filled me up before lifting the bowl to my face for a closer inspection. Odd was right; it did smell unusual. Unusually disgusting, that is. Like something you might find swimming about at the bottom of a rubbish bin, at first glance it appeared to be nothing more than a watery mush. At second glance, however, it was a watery mush with the occasional stringy bit stuck to the side and numerous misshapen lumps bobbing up and down on the surface.

'What is this?' I whispered.

'Soup,' replied Dodge.

'Really?' I screwed up my face, not entirely convinced. 'What kind of soup?'

'Horrible soup,' grinned Wheelie. 'I don't know why I'm smiling. We have to drink it now.'

'*Eat* it,' said Mo, correcting him. 'You don't drink soup.'

Holding his nose, Wheelie raised it to his lips. 'It's still revolting, however you get it down you—'

'Silence,' said Odd sternly. 'This is not the time to talk –

this is the time to feast! Ah, here's mine …'

I peered up from my bowl, half-expecting to see that Odd had one of his own.

Wow! How wrong could I be?

To my amazement, Norman had appeared with another trolley. This one, though, was piled high with food. Proper food. Food you could actually eat. Cream cakes, cookies and custard slices were sat side by side with sponges, strudels and other sweet treats that didn't begin with a *c* or an *s*. Hey, there was even a healthy option. I could see an apple or two, a bunch of bananas and a handful of grapes balanced precariously on the edge of the trolley, ready to fall off if Norman hit one bump too many.

I peered around the circle. All the other children were greedily slurping up their soup. Even Dodge, Wheelie, Mo and Angel. It may have sickened me, but I certainly wasn't surprised. The children looked famished. Absolutely starving. Prepared to eat anything, however disgusting it was.

I turned my attention to Odd. Sat cross-legged on the rug, he had started to stuff as much food into his mouth as he could possibly manage. He didn't even appear to care what it was. If it was sweet and sugary it was going in. That was all that mattered.

I had seen enough.

Placing the bowl by my feet, I pushed it firmly across the ground. 'I'm not eating that!' I remarked.

'Pardon?' Odd lifted his head and looked over at me. 'Did you say something, Twenty?'

'I'm not eating that,' I repeated, gesturing towards the bowl. 'Whatever it is, it shouldn't end up in your stomach. It shouldn't even end up in a sewer!'

Odd wiped his hands on a napkin before he stood up. 'Who do you think you are?' he raged. 'How dare you come here ... to my island ... and—'

'I didn't come here to your island!' I argued. 'You kidnapped me! There's a difference. And now I want to go home. We all do.'

'That's not going to happen,' spat Odd. 'Never. If you're going to be accepted here, Twenty, you need to change your ways.'

'And that's not going to happen either,' I shouted back at him. 'There's more chance of me changing my underpants than my ways.'

A combination of gasps and giggles rang out around the circle.

'Why are you doing this?' asked Odd, shaking his head at me. 'Why can't you just be happy like the rest of my children?'

'Happy?' I snorted. 'Do they look happy? At least a third of them are crying!'

I felt something pull on my boiler suit. It was Wheelie. 'A quarter,' he whispered.

I screwed up my face. 'What?'

'A quarter of them are crying,' Wheelie explained. 'All the Sobbers. That's five out of twenty. A quarter. You don't need to go to school to figure that out.'

'Right ... a *quarter* of them are crying,' I said, correcting myself as I turned back to Odd. 'They don't like it here. Nobody does. And they don't like *you*.'

'They don't like me?' Odd pressed a hand to his heart as if he had been shot. 'That's not true, is it, my children?'

The circle fell deathly silent. Odd gave it a few seconds before he spoke again.

'See,' he sneered. 'But, yes, you're right. They don't like me … because they *love* me! They all do. Every last one of them … except you.' I was about to reply when Odd pressed a finger to his lips. 'Enough of your nastiness,' he hissed. 'You've upset both me and my children and that will never do. I know there's a good boy hidden inside you somewhere, Twenty, but he's struggling to get out. I won't give up on you, though. If you don't know how to behave, then I must be the one to teach you. You will learn … but you will learn the hard way.'

I guessed the *hard way* was Norman. I glanced over at him, but he was still yet to move.

'No, not my special boy,' said Odd, following my gaze. 'I've got another idea. Something a little more embarrassing. Something to put you in your place once and for all.' Odd sat back down on the rug and picked up a cookie. 'You've asked for it, Twenty,' he said, grinning at me, 'and now you're going to get it!'

16.'FEELING HUNGRY?'

Ebenezer Odd looked around the circle.

'Three … Seven … Ten … Fifteen … Seventeen,' he called out. 'Will you please step forward.'

I watched as the Savages sat across from me began to rise up off the ground.

'If Twenty refuses to eat my delicious soup then maybe he'd like to try something else,' Odd remarked. 'A *lot* of something else. Do I make myself clear?'

Four of the children simply nodded, but the biggest of them, the boy with the spiky hair who had run his finger across his throat only moments earlier, chose to speak.

'Sure thing, Daddy,' he replied. 'You can rely on us.'

'Very good, Three,' said Odd, smiling back at him. 'How long would you like? A minute?'

The boy called Three shook his head. 'Two.'

'As you wish,' said Odd. 'You have two minutes. Starting from now …'

I jumped to my feet as Three rushed forwards. Then I relaxed a little as he turned sharply and veered towards Odd's sweet trolley. To my surprise, he started to collect as much food as he could possibly carry. At the same time, the other four Savages began to circle me.

'I'm not watching,' said Odd, covering his eyes. 'Violence always makes my tummy turn.'

I was still focussing on Three when two of the other Savages – a boy and a girl – tried to grab me by my arms. I pushed them away one at a time. That was easier than I expected. If I thought I had done enough, though, I was sadly mistaken. Before I knew it, the other two Savages had joined in as well. Now I had four of them to contend with. They moved as one and I couldn't fight them off. I was going down … and there was nothing I could do about it!

I hit the ground face-first as the Savages piled on top of me. Two of them put their weight on my arms, whilst the other two gripped hold of my ankles. There was no point struggling. All I could do was lay there, flat on my stomach with my chin on the ground, and see what happened next.

And what happened next was bizarre to say the least. Crouching down beside me, the boy called Three placed the pile of food in front of my nose before whispering in my ear.

'I'm Buck,' he snarled. 'Remember the name because you'll be hearing a lot more of it from now on. I run this place. Odd Island is mine … and no skinny little squirt like you is going to change that!'

'I wouldn't dream of it,' I muttered. At the same time, Buck grabbed a doughnut. For a moment I thought he might stick it in his mouth and eat it in full view of me.

Unfortunately, I couldn't have been more wrong …

'Feeling hungry?' he asked.

'I was,' I admitted. 'Not so much now. Although I've a bad feeling you're about to—'

My sentence was cut short when Buck thrust the doughnut between my lips. I almost swallowed it whole before managing, somehow, to spit it out across the ground.

'Ungrateful,' smirked Buck. 'Oh, was it too sweet for you? How about a piece of fruit instead?'

I was about to object when Buck shoved a whole banana – skin and all – into my mouth. It touched the back of my throat and I began to gag. I don't know how but, using a combination of my tongue and teeth, I was able to push it out.

'Muffin?' asked Buck, picking one up off the ground. 'Two muffins? Three muffins?'

I snapped my jaw shut before the spiky-haired Savage could force-feed me anything else.

'Don't be like that, Twenty,' said Buck, grinning manically. 'Open wide like a good little number.'

I kept my teeth clenched firmly together as he tried to force his fingers into my mouth. It shocked me when he gave in without too much of a fight. I was less shocked, however, when he squeezed my nostrils together. 'Got to breathe eventually,' Buck sniggered.

He was right, of course. The horror of what was happening had left me exhausted. I couldn't hold my breath forever.

Buck refused to wait and tried to squeeze a muffin into a gap that didn't exist. Fearing for my teeth, I opened my mouth just a fraction. The muffin was in before I knew it.

My cheeks bulged and I started to frantically chew. Thankfully, it was soft and squidgy.

'One minute,' called out Odd. 'I'm not watching. I promise.'

I felt weaker than weak as the last of the muffin either disappeared down my throat or fell from my lips. Laid on my stomach, it was almost impossible for me to swallow. Not that Buck seemed to care. The food was coming so fast now it was just a blur. I didn't have the strength to resist or the time to chew as Buck pushed more and more inside my mouth. All I could do was hope that it would end. And preferably before I choked.

A loud scream changed everything.

It wasn't coming from me, but it was close enough for me to think that it could've been. All of a sudden I felt the pressure ease on my body. The weight on my arms vanished and there was nobody gripping hold of my ankles.

I was free to move.

Food fell from my mouth as I scrambled to my feet. Buck backed away in shock, giving me just enough time to look behind me. To my amazement, the four other Savages had been taken out in ways I would never have imagined possible. Wheelie had dealt with one by rolling his wheelchair over their feet, pinning them beneath him. Dodge had gone one step further by wrestling another to the ground, whilst Mo had gone one step further than that by sitting on a third. Sitting on their head, that is.

The fourth, however, a boy, was hopping about in the middle of the circle, his arms wrapped around his body. It was him that had screamed. And with good reason, too.

Something was missing … and that something was his boiler suit!

I spotted it screwed up in a heap by Angel's feet. I had no idea how she had done it but, somehow, she had removed it from his body. Now he was completely naked except for his underpants. And that meant he was no longer a threat.

Four down … but there was still one Savage to go.

And this one was mine.

Buck was a different boy now. With the other Savages out of action, he was no longer so full of himself. Yes, he was still twice my size, but the odds were equal. No, you're right. They weren't equal at all.

One spy against one big bully was never going to be a fair fight, was it?

Buck came at me, waving a chocolate log above his head. I held my ground and waited … and waited … and waited … before crouching down. As Buck swung wildly above me, I tucked my head into my shoulders and rolled over. Like a human bowling ball, I took him out at the ankles. His legs buckled and he fell forwards, landing heavily amongst the wasted food he had tried to force into my mouth. At the same time, I grabbed a cream cake from the pile and splattered it straight into Buck's face before he had a chance to recover.

'Times up.' Odd was smiling when he first removed his hands. And then he wasn't. 'What happened?' he cried.

'He *happened*, Daddy,' whined Buck, wiping the cream from his eyes. 'Twenty. He's to blame for everything.'

'He did all this?' gasped Odd, staring at me in disbelief. I stared back at him, wondering what he was going to do next. When he finally acted, however, it took me by surprise. 'Lunch is over, my children,' he announced. 'Now tidy this mess and get on with your chores.'

I watched as Ebenezer Odd shuffled off towards the Nerve Centre without another word. I half-expected him to turn around and say something to me. Some kind of warning perhaps. Or a threat.

He didn't.

Instead, he pulled open the door and disappeared inside without breaking stride. He was out of sight.

Out of sight … but never out of mind.

17.'YOU WOULDN'T WANT TO HURT YOURSELF.'

I was still gazing at the Nerve Centre when Wheelie rolled over my toes.

'Take this,' he said, handing me a long, wooden brush. 'You can help me sweep up. I normally start at the fence and work my way around the compound.'

'Sounds good to me,' I said. I mean, it didn't. It sounded terrible. But that wasn't enough to stop me from following my new friend as he moved towards the edge of the courtyard.

'Don't get too close to the fence,' remarked Wheelie. He stopped without warning and I walked straight into his wheelchair. 'You'll get electrocuted if you touch it.'

'Been there, done that,' I sighed. 'Or something similar at least.'

'Ah, you mean the child zapper,' nodded Wheelie. 'Given half a chance I'd ram it right up Odd's ...' He broke off suddenly and glanced nervously over his shoulder. 'If Norman sees that we're not working he'll come over and give us a shove. Just push your brush around whilst we talk. That's all I ever do. Oh, don't look now, but somebody seems to be giving you daggers ...'

What a ridiculous thing to say! Of course I was going to look.

I began to sweep the ground, but let my gaze shift across the courtyard as I did so. Wheelie was right. Knelt down where we had once been sat, Buck's hands may have been busy clearing up the wasted food, but his eyes were glaring straight at me.

'You're not very good at making friends, are you?' Wheelie remarked. 'First Odd and now Buck. He thinks he's the top dog around here. He won't be happy that you made a fool of him back there.'

'He started it,' I insisted.

'And then you finished it,' grinned Wheelie.

'Someone had to,' I shrugged. 'You know the old saying. The harder they come, the harder they fall ...'

'The harder they fall ... the more likely they are to come again,' Wheelie added. 'And next time he'll be even angrier than he was today. I hope you're ready, Hugo. No, don't tell me. You were born ready.'

'No, I was born a baby,' I said, correcting him. 'We all are. I thought everybody knew that.'

Wheelie stopped sweeping and studied me for a moment. 'There's something about you,' he began. 'You're not ... normal.'

'It's my face, isn't it?' I said. 'Just try not to look at me when you're about to eat—'

'Don't change the subject,' said Wheelie. 'I saw the way you took out Buck. You've got skills. Ordinary kids can't do that. So, what are you? Surely you're not a ... hey!'

Wheelie yelped out loud as his whole body began to shudder. Without either of us noticing, Ebenezer Odd's special boy had crept up behind him and grabbed the handles of his wheelchair.

'Work,' Norman grunted.

I put my head down and ran the brush across the ground, sweeping the dust and debris between the cracks in the fence. I waited for Norman to leave before I started to count. I made it all the way to thirty-seven seconds ... and then started to speak on thirty-eight.

'What's out there?' I asked, gesturing beyond the fence.

'Fog,' said Wheelie. 'But then you can see that for yourself, can't you? After that it's hard to tell. If we're on an island then we must be surrounded by water. Makes sense, right? Some of the others reckon there are trees out there. Like a forest. They say you can make out the top of the branches if you look hard enough.'

I tried to do just that, but couldn't see much beyond the fog.

'You can't escape that way if that's what you're thinking,' remarked Wheelie.

'It wasn't,' I said honestly. 'But it is now. Why can't I?'

'The fog's impenetrable,' Wheelie explained. 'Thicker than thick.'

'Like Buck?' I said.

'No, thicker than that,' laughed Wheelie. 'There's no way through. You'll just get lost.'

I screwed up my face. 'Who told you that? Not Odd?'

'No,' replied Wheelie. 'Well, maybe. I can't remember. But it is common knowledge around here.'

'Just because Odd tells you something it doesn't mean it's true,' I argued.

Wheelie didn't have an answer for that. 'Do you know about the wild wolves?' he asked instead. 'They're everywhere. That's why we have the fence and the guards. To stop them from getting in.'

I raised an eyebrow. Odd had told me that as well. He had probably told everyone that when they had first arrived. Once again, however, it didn't mean it was necessarily true.

'What's up?' asked Wheelie. 'By the look on your face you're either deep in thought or else you've stepped too close to the fence and been ... whoa!'

Wheelie cried out in horror as Norman shook his wheelchair for a second time. I don't know how he had done it, but, once again, he had successfully sneaked up without either of us realising.

'Split,' ordered Norman, gesturing for us to part. I did as he asked and moved away from Wheelie. I began to sweep but, this time, Norman didn't leave me to it. Instead, he followed me around the perimeter of the compound, staring blindly into space.

Seconds turned to minutes. Minutes turned to hours. And hours turned to ... no, don't overdo it, Hugo. I wasn't out there that long. But it *was* dark by the time a bell sounded. That was the signal for us to stop working. At least, that was what I assumed when all the other children hurried back to their huts.

Shielding my eyes from the searchlights, I glanced up at the watchtower as I wandered past. The guards were still there, stood to attention. As far as I could tell they hadn't moved all day.

I had almost made it all the way to the hut when I heard a voice. 'Give.'

I turned around slowly. I had been hoping that Norman wouldn't have noticed that I was still carrying the sweeping brush, but clearly he had. Shame. As weapons go, it was as good as any.

'Oh, my mistake,' I said, walking back down the ramp. Norman snatched wildly at the brush, but missed completely and ended up stumbling. 'Careful,' I said, lifting my free hand to steady him. 'You wouldn't want to hurt yourself.'

Norman pushed me away before making another grab for the brush. This time, however, I moved it out of the way on purpose.

'What's wrong?' I asked. 'Is it your eyes? Can't you see properly?'

'Home,' ordered Norman, pointing at the hut.

'No, I'm a long way from home,' I replied. 'But this isn't about me – it's about you. I'm here to help.'

Clenching his fists, Norman stomped towards me.

'Don't be like that,' I said, backing away from him. 'I'm worried about you. Well, your eyes at least. I think you might need glasses.'

'Glasses?' Norman put his hands up to his face. 'Glasses?' he repeated.

'Glasses will help you see better,' I explained. 'You should ask Odd to get you some. You are his special boy, after all. And he wouldn't want to see you unhappy now, would he?'

Norman began to frown. 'Unhappy.'

'If you're unhappy you should do something about it,' I continued. I was pushing my luck, but there was still one last point I wanted to get across before I headed back to the hut. 'Listen, Norman, you don't have to be the bad guy all the time. And you don't have to do everything Odd tells you. Think about it. I would if I was you.'

I had almost made it to the hut when Norman spoke again. 'Give.'

I looked down at the brush and then held it out for Norman to take. Striding forwards, he grabbed it first time before deliberately barging into me, knocking me off balance.

'No glasses,' he said firmly. He pushed me again and then walked away.

I steadied myself before I made sure I had the final word. 'It's your choice,' I called out. 'If you need any more advice you know where to find me.'

With that, I pulled open the door and hurried inside before Norman could barge into me for a second time.

'Where have you been?' asked Wheelie.

'Just making friends,' I said, winking at him. I closed the door behind me before I let my eyes dart around the hut. I found Angel sat on the bucket in the corner. That meant I was safe to talk. 'Thanks for everything you did out there,' I said. 'You know, with the Savages. If it wasn't for you lot I'd most probably be dead by now. Dead from over-eating.'

'Think nothing of it, matey,' said Dodge, patting me on the shoulder.

'Buck and his band of bruisers have been asking for that for ages,' said Mo fiercely.

'I'd even go as far as to say it's the most fun we've had since we've been here,' remarked Wheelie. 'Quite exciting really.'

'Th–Th–Thank you,' stuttered Angel. She smiled at me so I smiled back. I was still smiling, in fact, when Wheelie prodded me with one of his crutches.

'Sit down,' he said. 'You make the place look untidy.'

I did as he suggested and sat down beside him. 'What now?' I wondered.

'Now we wait,' sighed Mo.

I screwed up my face. 'Wait? What for?'

The door to the hut flew open before anyone could reply.

'For *this*,' groaned Mo, resting her head against her pillow. 'It's the One we've all been waiting for.'

18.'I'LL SCREAM!'

If you had asked me who it was who had burst into the hut I would've guessed at Norman.

And I would've been wrong.

It was, in fact, a particularly small girl with blonde curly hair, sticky-out ears and a dimple on her chin. She was huffing and puffing as she struggled to drag four grey sacks behind her. I stood up, ready to help, when the girl turned to me in disgust.

'I don't like you,' she blurted out.

I glanced over my shoulder just to be certain. Yes, she *was* talking to me.

'Bit rude,' I replied, sitting back down again. 'You don't even know me.'

'I know enough,' sneered the girl. 'You're an absolute horror. It's boys like you that ruin Odd Island for the rest of us.'

'It's girls like you who make Odd Island so unbearable to begin with,' I muttered to myself.

The girl either didn't hear or chose to ignore me. 'I'm One,' she said snootily. 'Daddy's favourite.'

'Also known as Prissy Priscilla,' added Wheelie. 'The Queen of the Suck-ups.'

'Don't call me that, you wicked worm,' cried Priscilla. 'I'll tell Daddy. You know he doesn't like it when his children are beastly to one another.'

'He didn't seem to mind when he set the Savages on me,' I grumbled.

'That was your own fault,' Priscilla insisted. 'You needed to be taught a lesson. And you were—'

'No, I wasn't,' I argued.

'Maybe Daddy would like to know that, too,' said Priscilla. 'There's always Isolation for boys like you who need to learn the hard way.'

I didn't like the sound of that. 'Isolation?'

'Oh dear, Twenty.' Priscilla began to smile. 'You didn't think you could just carry on being ghastly and get away with it forever, did you? No, before you know it Daddy will stick you somewhere you can't cause any trouble. Isolation is a lot like prison. Except it's darker and smaller and smellier and—'

'How would you know?' argued Mo. 'You've never been there.'

'No, but I've heard the stories,' replied Priscilla smugly. 'Zero was taken to Isolation weeks ago and he still hasn't come back yet. Is that what you want, Twenty? What's wrong? You don't seem so sure of yourself anymore.'

I didn't like to admit it, but she had a point. I had been sent to Odd Island to find the children and rescue them, even the likes of Priscilla and Buck. I was halfway there, but how was I supposed to do the rescuing bit if I was locked up?

'Okay, Priscilla, you're boring us now,' snapped Mo. 'Just do what you've got to do and get out.'

'I'll leave when I'm ready,' said Priscilla stubbornly. There was an awkward silence. 'And I'm ready now,' she announced, much to everyone's relief.

With that, she lifted one of the grey sacks and tipped it out over Wheelie's bed, not far from where I was sat. I stood up so I could study its contents. It was mainly scraps and leftovers.

'Why are you dumping all that rubbish in here?' I moaned.

'That's not rubbish,' sniggered Priscilla. 'That's dinner. And, if you ask me, it's more than you deserve.'

She turned to leave, but then turned back just as suddenly when something caught her eye.

No, not something. Someone.

Angel.

'I see you sitting on the bucket, Eighteen,' said Priscilla, jabbing a finger in her direction. 'You know Daddy doesn't like us to have private conversations.'

'I'm s-s-sorry,' mumbled Angel.

'Don't be,' said Mo, frowning at her. 'We all do it. Even the Queen of the Suck-ups.'

'Maybe I do,' shrugged Priscilla, 'but then *I* would never say anything horrible about Daddy behind his back. Unlike you lot. Maybe I should tell him what you get up to when you're left to your own devices.'

'I've had enough of this.' Dodge moved swiftly to block

the door. 'You can try and tell Odd …'

'… But you'll have to get out of here first,' finished Mo, clenching her fists.

An increasingly anxious Priscilla looked around the hut at all the angry faces. 'I'll scream!' she cried. 'And I won't stop until Norman comes and finds me—'

'Whoa! Whoa! There's no need for any of this,' I said, raising my hands. 'Falling out and arguing isn't going to help anyone. Thanks for dinner, One. We're all extremely grateful. No, I'm being serious. It looks absolutely … erm … I can't quite think how best to describe it—'

'Shut up, you awful boy!' spat Priscilla.

'Yes, awful,' I said, nodding at her. 'That's the word I'm looking for.'

Priscilla spun around to leave. At the same time, something fell from her pocket and landed by my feet.

'Wait,' I said, bending down to pick it up. 'You seem to have dropped—'

'Don't touch that!' Priscilla snatched it from my grasp before I had a chance to react. 'It's my pass,' she revealed. 'Once the doors lock at seven o'clock it's the only way to get around the compound.'

'I don't understand,' I admitted.

'You wouldn't,' spat Priscilla, waving the pass in my face. 'This opens every door in every building. It gets me into all four huts and the Nerve Centre. Only Daddy's favourites are allowed one. And, yes, that means me!'

'Interesting.' I shifted to one side as Priscilla picked up the remaining grey sacks. 'So long, One,' I said, opening the door for her. 'See you soon.'

'Hopefully not,' muttered Priscilla, pushing past me on her way out.

I waited until the door had closed before I turned back into the hut. 'She seems nice,' I said, shaking my head at the same time.

'Anyone fancy a slice of mouldy bread and … and …' Wheelie held up something brown and lumpy from the pile Priscilla had dropped on his bed. 'I'm not being deliberately revolting,' he began, 'but the last time I saw one of these it was floating about in a toilet.'

'Ugh! Gross!' moaned Mo. 'I'm not eating that.'

'You don't have to,' I blurted out. Things were starting to take shape. I knew it wouldn't be easy, but, with a little bit of brain power, I was sure I could figure something out.

'I can see those clogs turning, matey,' said Dodge, grinning at me. He was right. And the more the clogs turned, the more the pieces slotted smoothly into place. 'You're planning something,' Dodge remarked.

'Sounds good to me,' said Wheelie, tossing the bread to one side. 'What are you thinking, Hugo?'

'I'm thinking we need Priscilla's pass,' I replied. 'And I know just the way to get it.'

19.'OPERATION PASS SNATCH IS GO ... GO ... GO!'

I told everybody in the hut what I had in mind.

And nobody argued. I know. Crazy, right? I mean, you'd think at least one of them would have objected and said it was too dangerous. Or too foolish. Or both dangerously foolish and foolishly dangerous. Yeah, that sounds a lot like me. But, no, I had spoken, they had listened and then they had all agreed.

Wow.

I sat back down before I fell down. I wasn't used to people agreeing with me. If anything, it made me feel a little light-headed.

'If this is going to work then we have to move quickly,' insisted Wheelie. Pushing himself up, he tried to slide from his bed to his wheelchair, fully aware that one wrong move would mean he fell through the ever-increasing gap between the two of them. Dodge offered to help, but Wheelie waved him away. 'I can do it on my own,' he snapped. A second later he was true to his word. 'Sorry,' he said, catching his breath. 'I wasn't ... I'm not ... it's just—'

'It doesn't matter, matey,' Dodge shrugged.

'Yes, it does,' insisted Wheelie. 'You were only trying to help. I know that. The thing is … sometimes I like to do things for myself. I never get the chance at home, you see. My mum and dad … my sister … they all just fuss around me. I know they're only being nice, but …' Wheelie ended that particular sentence with a loud sigh. 'That's why I'm so keen to put this plan into action,' he said, rubbing his hands together. 'It's not often I get a lead role in anything this exciting. I won't let you down.'

'I'm sure you won't.' I followed Wheelie as he rolled towards the exit. 'Do any of you want me to go over things one more time?' I asked.

'I'd rather you didn't,' muttered Mo. 'It was boring enough the first time you told us.'

'I think that's a *no*, matey,' said Dodge. He cautiously opened the door and peeked outside. The smart move would've been for us to hold tight and wait for him to report back, but that was never going to happen. Instead, we all forced our way to the front for a better view of the courtyard. By the time we had finished, the door was wide open and Dodge had been bundled over.

I had no idea what time it was, but figured it must be early evening. Five or six o'clock perhaps. Mo had told me that the door to the hut locked at seven so it wasn't that late. What I couldn't understand, though, was why it didn't feel any chillier out there. Back in Crooked Elbow it had been the middle of winter. Things got cold after dark. *Seriously* cold. Freezing even. And yet the temperature on Odd Island was anything but. The air was mild and it was a wind-free zone.

Where was I? Was I even in the same country? On the same continent? On the same … *gulp* … planet?

Relax, Hugo. Ebenezer Odd might be weird, but he's not an alien. Norman, however …

'Budge, you guys.' Careful not to draw attention, Wheelie manoeuvred the wheelchair until he found himself at the top of the ramp. 'I'm ready to roll,' he whispered.

Priscilla had left our hut five minutes ago. Or four. Or six. I hadn't been counting so I couldn't be certain. Regardless, there was no way whatsoever she would have finished her drop-offs already. We were the first hut she had visited and she still had three more huts after that. Dinner – if you could call it that – had not yet been served to everybody.

'What about the guards?' asked Dodge, shielding his eyes from the searchlights. 'We can't just stand here on the doorstep. We look … dodgy.'

'Yes, *you* do,' I said, grinning at him. 'Dodge by name, dodgy by nature. The rest of us, however, look fine. Besides, it's not as if we're doing anything wrong. Well, we are, but that's our little secret. For all the guards know we're just taking in the sights … breathing in the fresh air. There's nothing suspicious about that.'

'Course not,' grumbled Mo. 'What could be more enjoyable than thick fog, wild wolves and an electric fence? It's the holiday I've always dreamt of.'

'That's the spirit,' I said, patting her on the back. 'I like your positivity.'

'I was being sarcastic,' Mo groaned.

'So was I,' I replied. 'You should stop being so grumpy, Maureen. It doesn't suit you.'

Mo turned and grabbed me by the scruff of my boiler suit. 'Do not call me Maureen—'

'Cut it out, you two,' said Dodge. He stopped and pointed across the courtyard. 'Look!'

Priscilla was coming out of one of the other huts, but now there was only one sack left. I guessed that was for her and the rest of the Suck-ups. If we let her vanish inside her own hut now we would have missed our chance.

'This is it,' I said. 'Operation Pass Snatch is go … go … go!'

'Consider me gone.' With that, Wheelie released the brake on his wheelchair. Pushing himself off, he began to roll down the ramp, picking up speed with every rotation. Before I knew it, he was hurtling across the courtyard. That was the easy bit, though. Now he had to put his acting skills to the test.

'I can't stop!' Wheelie called out. 'My brakes … they've failed!'

They hadn't, of course. It was all part of the plan. Not that Priscilla knew that. From what I could see, the shout seemed to have both shocked and stopped her.

'Out of the way!' yelled Wheelie, swerving from side-to-side.

Priscilla had frozen with panic. She was rooted to the spot.

'Don't just stand there!' screamed Wheelie, pretending

to lose control as he deliberately veered towards her. 'Move!'

And, finally, she did. Panic-stricken or not, Priscilla still managed to defrost enough to skip ever so slightly to one side.

But then Wheelie moved too. Priscilla was still in his sights and the wheelchair was back on course.

On course for a courtyard collision.

Wheelie waited until the very last moment before he stamped down on the foot plates and applied the brakes. As expected, the wheelchair skidded across the ground before it struck Priscilla. Thankfully, it was nothing more than a glancing blow. Not hard enough to hurt her, but still enough to knock her off her feet. Wheelie followed her lead and rolled out of his seat. By the time he had settled he was face down on the ground with an upturned wheelchair left stranded beside him. He looked in pain. But looks can be deceptive. Wheelie was fine. I was sure of it.

As acting goes, that was up there with the best.

I nudged Angel. 'Your turn.'

She didn't need telling twice. Running down the ramp, she started quietly but then built up until she was squealing at the top of her voice. It was an horrendous racket, like twelve cats stuck up a tree, begging to be rescued. It was also exactly what I had asked her to do. And more besides.

Things were going to plan.

I hadn't been on Odd Island long, but it was still long enough to know that Odd's special boy would be first on the scene. This time, however, he would arrive exactly when I wanted, not when he chose to.

Any … second … Norman.

Right on cue, the door to the Nerve Centre flew open and out marched the most monumental meathead I had ever had the misfortune to bump into.

I turned to Mo and Dodge and gave them a nod. 'Your turn.'

This was the tricky part of the plan. If it wasn't timed to perfection then it wouldn't work. And if it didn't work then it would all be for nothing. And if it was all for nothing then I would probably have to creep back into our hut and pretend it wasn't my idea in the first place.

I crossed my fingers as Norman set off at pace towards the mess that was Wheelie and Priscilla. What he didn't see, however, were Mo and Dodge running across the courtyard. They were coming up on his blindside. One at the front and one at the back.

Double trouble.

Norman had almost reached the wheelchair when Mo crashed straight into him. From a distance, it looked like an accident. Nothing more, nothing less. Dodge, meanwhile, crouched down behind him at the exact same moment. Norman, naturally, staggered backwards when Mo bounced off him … and then tripped over Dodge.

Daddy's special boy was down … but certainly not out.

Shielding my eyes, I peered up at the guards in the watchtower. They hadn't moved. Not even an inch. Which probably meant that they hadn't seen what was happening.

Move, Hugo. Move.

Racing down the ramp, I winked at Angel and she

screamed even louder. Norman still hadn't got up by the time I reached the wheelchair, but he was the least of my worries.

It was Priscilla who I was interested in.

Leaning over her, I used one hand to help her to her feet, whilst the other wasn't quite so innocent and slipped into her pocket instead. If the pass was going to be anywhere, it was there.

'Get off me, you revolting creature,' shrieked Priscilla, pushing me away.

At the same time my fingers brushed against something small and flat. It had to be the pass. I snatched at it blindly and held on tight as I began to stumble backwards. Quick as a flash, I dropped it into my own pocket before I had even bothered to steady myself. It had worked. My plan, I mean. I had done it. No, *we* had done it. We had really done it.

Or maybe not …

I was all set to leave the scene of the crime when I sensed movement behind me. There was someone there. Closer than close. I glanced over my shoulder, fearing the worst.

The worst being Norman.

But it wasn't. It was Angel.

I was about to say something when Ebenezer Odd beat me to it.

'What is going on out here?' he cried. Closing the door to the Nerve Centre behind him, he put his head down and hurried across the courtyard.

'Nothing, Daddy,' I said, trying not to look in any way suspicious as I helped Wheelie back into his chair. 'It was just an accident.'

'I'm not sure I can trust you,' said Odd, scowling at me. 'Maybe my special boy would be kind enough to fill me in …'

There was a moment's silence whilst Norman strained his brain for an answer.

'Accident,' he shrugged eventually.

'In that case, back to your dormitories,' ordered Odd, seemingly satisfied. 'All of you. There's nothing to see here.'

Mo and Dodge couldn't believe their luck and rushed back up the ramp and into the hut before Odd could change his mind. To my surprise, Angel was already waiting for them.

Now it was my turn.

'We're already on our way, Daddy,' I said, grabbing the wheelchair by its handles.

'You don't have to push me,' muttered Wheelie under his breath.

'I'm not doing it for you – I'm doing it for me!' I insisted. 'I just want to get back to the hut as quickly as possible.'

'Why didn't you say so?' Right on cue, Wheelie pushed on his wheels and he sped off. He was moving so fast I could barely keep up.

Then it happened. The one thing I feared most.

'My pass!' screeched Priscilla. 'It's been stolen!'

Wheelie rolled straight up the ramp and into the hut. I was right behind him.

'What do you mean, One?' asked Odd.

Dodge was stood by the door, holding it open for me. I was almost there.

'I can't find it,' whined Priscilla. 'I had it ... I know I did ... and now ... it's gone!'

Dodge held out his hand. I was about to grab it and dive inside when Odd stopped me dead in my tracks.

'Come back here, Twenty,' he shouted. 'I haven't finished with you yet.'

20.'I'M A GOOD BOY.'

I turned slowly and set off down the ramp.

There were only three people left in the courtyard now.

Ebenezer Odd.

Norman.

And Priscilla.

If I'm being honest, not one of them looked particularly pleased to see me.

I slowed my step and, ever so gently, stroked my fingers against the outside of my pocket. That was where I had put the pass. If I couldn't find it now and I had lost it then it would all be for nothing.

'Put your hands in the air!' snapped Odd. 'Don't touch anything!'

I reluctantly did as I was told, none the wiser as to whether the pass was still there. 'What seems to be the problem, Daddy?' I asked innocently.

'*You*, Twenty,' replied Odd. 'You're the problem. Something has vanished and you appear to have been right in the middle of things at the time of the occurrence.'

'I'd call that a coincidence,' I shrugged.

'I wouldn't,' argued Odd. 'One's pass has gone missing—'

'And you'd like me to search for it,' I said, finishing his sentence. Dropping down onto my hands and knees, I pressed my nose to the ground and began to sniff. 'You've made a good choice, Daddy,' I said, glancing up at him. 'I'm the best searcher on the whole of Odd Island. I'm like a dog without a bone. Because if I had the bone I wouldn't need to keep searching, would I? I'd just stop and ... um ... enjoy the bone. Although, what enjoyment I could possibly get from a dry old bone I'll never know—'

'Silence in the courtyard!' Odd barked. 'I do not want you to search for a bone – I want you to give me the pass! I know you've got it.'

I screwed up my face. 'Do you?'

'Yes, I do,' insisted Odd. 'I'm sure of it.'

'Are you really?' I said.

'Yes, I am,' snapped Odd. 'Stop asking questions, Twenty. This is not a game.'

'Isn't it?' I replied.

Odd's brow began to furrow. 'What are you doing?'

I was playing for time, of course. Not that I'd ever tell Odd that. And it wasn't as if he could read my mind.

'You're playing for time,' remarked Odd. Oh. Ignore that last comment. 'Check him all over, my special boy. Twenty has the pass and I want you to find it.'

I tensed up as Norman pulled me towards him and began to pat me down.

'Why do you think I've got it?' I asked, trying to keep calm. 'I'm a good boy.'

'Only half of that statement is true,' snorted Odd. 'It's not difficult to guess which half.'

'No, I don't suppose it is,' I shrugged. 'But if I'm not a boy, what am I?'

The words died on my lips as Norman stuffed a hand into my pocket.

'You seem to have gone very quiet, Twenty,' remarked Odd suspiciously.

It was only when Norman removed his hand that I felt capable of breathing. He had drawn a blank. He hadn't found a thing. Which, whether I liked it or not, was both good and bad. Yes, he had failed to find the pass, but if it wasn't in my pocket, where was it? 'I thought you'd prefer me to be quiet,' I replied.

'I'd prefer it if you told me where you'd hidden the pass.' A frustrated-looking Odd switched his attention to Norman. 'Flip him over, my special boy,' he demanded.

I was about to ask what he meant by that when Norman lifted me off the ground and turned me upside down by my ankles. Now I was just hanging in mid-air, powerless to fight back as the blood rushed to my head.

'Shake him all over, my special boy,' ordered Odd. 'Let's see what comes out.'

I didn't have time to protest as Norman did exactly what he was told. My eyes began to blur as every part of my body shuddered. The only thing that was likely to come out, though, was all that food that Buck had tried to force-feed me a few hours ago.

'Spin him around, my special boy,' urged Odd.

Norman started to turn on the spot, faster and faster and faster. Like the world's worst fairground ride, my stomach began to do more somersaults than I could count. This couldn't go on forever ...

'Drop him, my special boy,' commanded Odd.

Yes, I wanted it to stop ... but certainly not like that. A second later Norman let go of my ankles and I flew across the courtyard. With no time to spare, I lowered my hands and tried to soften the blow of landing. Yes, I hit the ground hard, but nowhere near as hard as I had expected.

'Back to your dormitory,' ordered Odd. 'You do not have the pass.'

'I told you that ages ago,' I moaned.

'I told you that ages ago ... *Daddy*.' With that, Odd turned his back on me. I was no longer of interest to him. Which was exactly what I wanted.

The pain was starting to ease so I climbed to my feet and walked wearily towards the hut. I could hear Odd lecturing Priscilla about being so careless, whilst Norman continued to search frantically for the missing pass. Not that he would ever find it, of course. There was only one person who knew where it really was. And that was me.

Or so I hoped.

I held my breath as I slipped my hand into my pocket and fumbled about. It didn't take me long to realise that I was wrong. I didn't know where the pass was. And that's because it wasn't there. It had gone.

I hesitated at the top of the ramp. The last thing I wanted to do now was head back inside the hut, but what choice did

I have? Just as I expected, the other Survivors were sat around in various places as I slipped through the door, each of them waiting eagerly for my return. Wheelie was on his bed, Mo was sat on the bucket, Angel was at the table and Dodge was on the floor with his back against the wall. It was him who spoke first.

'Have you still got the pass, matey?' he blurted out. 'Or did they find it?'

'Neither,' I muttered.

'Maybe I've got my wires crossed, but that doesn't make sense,' frowned Mo.

'No, it doesn't,' I shrugged. 'They didn't find it because it wasn't there. But it should've been. I took the pass from Priscilla and stuck it in my pocket. It must have fallen out, though, because—'

'It d-d-didn't fall out.' All eyes turned towards Angel. Pushing her chair to one side, she slowly stood up from the table and removed the pass from her own pocket. 'I t-t-took it from you.'

'You took it?' I repeated. 'From me?'

Angel nodded. There was a moment of stunned confusion before Dodge leapt to his feet and punched the air in celebration. Wheelie followed his lead and grabbed his crutches, twirling them wildly above his head. Even Mo was laughing now. So hard, in fact, that she had to steady herself in case she fell off the bucket.

Only Angel remained both still and silent.

'I've got no idea what happened out there,' said Mo, shaking her head in disbelief.

'I think I have.' I turned to face Angel. 'I remember now. You were behind me.'

'I p-p-picked your pockets,' remarked Angel, too embarrassed to look up from her feet. 'I th–th–thought it was the r–r–right thing to do.'

I paused. 'No, it wasn't the right thing to do,' I began. 'It was absolutely, unbelievably, no doubt about it, the best thing that anyone has ever done … and a tiny bit more after that!'

It was the first time I had seen it, but the slightest of smiles spread slowly across Angel's lips.

'This is f-f-for you,' she said, shuffling towards me so she could hand over the pass.

'But that means … the plan worked,' said Wheelie, struggling to catch his breath. 'It actually worked. Don't take it personally, but I never really thought it would …'

'No, me neither,' agreed Mo.

'Definitely not,' added Dodge.

Even Angel shrugged her shoulders.

'But it did,' continued Wheelie. 'We've got Priscilla's pass. So, what are we going to do with it?'

'*We're* not going to do anything with it,' I said. 'But *I* am. No, don't look at me like that, you lot. You haven't been fed properly in days. You're all weak. And I'm … not. Not yet, anyway. But I will be if this goes on much longer. Odd is starving us. He's trying to weaken us so we haven't got the strength to argue or fight back. I can't let that happen, though.' I stopped for breath. 'Leave this to me,' I insisted. 'I won't let you down.'

'Leave what to you?' wondered Mo.

'I'm going exploring,' I revealed. 'Not now. Later. When everybody's asleep. And I'll start with the kitchen.' I stopped to draw a breath. 'Tonight we feast like kings and queens, my friends,' I said, rubbing my hands together. 'Tonight we eat like Ebenezer Odd.'

21. 'YOU'RE OUR ONLY HOPE.'

We spent the rest of the evening talking.

Just nonsense really. Everything you can think of and nothing in particular. Chitter-chatter to take our minds off our current situation. It turned out that we all lived relatively close to one another, although not close enough to have ever met. We all went to different schools, but preferred it at the weekend when we didn't have to think about school at all. Dodge had just started boxing lessons because his dad wanted him to toughen up a little, Mo looked after horses in her spare time, and Wheelie was a keen artist. He used acrylics. I didn't even know what that meant, but nodded regardless. As for me, well, I told them I collected butterflies. I don't know why. It was the first thing that came to mind. Thankfully, no one questioned me. As the hours passed I learned a lot about each and every one of them. Oh, except Angel. As I had come to expect, she remained largely silent, but that was fine. Nobody was going to force her into speaking. Not if she didn't want to.

Naturally, it didn't take long for the conversation to shift back to Odd Island and the odious Ebenezer Odd. By the sound of things, the others had all been stuck there for somewhere between a week and a fortnight. Without a clock to look at, or any other way of telling the time, it was hard for them to be sure. Days just merged into one long blur. There was one thing they were certain of, though. They all wanted to go home. And I knew exactly how they felt. Yes, I had only been there a few hours, but it seemed like longer.

At some point the door had clicked, locking us in. Several hours later the lights went out and we were plunged into darkness. One by one, we drifted off to bed, trying (and failing) to make ourselves comfortable as we did so. The conversations continued, but now they were less personal and we didn't touch on anything that we didn't want Odd to hear. Some of the others slipped in and out of sleep, but not me. Spies don't sleep. That's a fact. Don't feel you have to remember that, though. Honestly. I'm about to tell you again in a few lines time so there's really no need.

'What t-t-time are you leaving?'

That was Angel. She may have barely spoken all evening, but now she had whispered the one question that I almost certainly needed to consider before it was too late.

'Hmm … about midnight,' I replied quietly. 'I think everybody should be asleep by then. Everybody except me. Because I don't sleep. Not today … not tomorrow … not the day after … never … ever … ever …'

My sentence mumbled to a halt a moment later. If I knew why I would tell you. But I don't. Sorry.

The next thing I knew somebody was gently shaking me. I couldn't be sure, but I figured they were trying to get my attention.

And it worked.

Leaping up off the bed, I clenched my fists and readied myself for an imminent attack. I relaxed a little when it didn't happen and then relaxed even more when my eyes adjusted and I saw that it was Angel who was knelt beside my bed.

'You made me jump,' I grumbled. 'What are you doing?'

'W-W-Waking you up,' revealed Angel.

'No, that's not possible,' I replied, shaking my head. 'You have to be asleep before you can be woken up. And I never sleep. Not ever. I told you that a few minutes ago.'

'No, you t-t-told me that a few *hours* ago,' said Angel, correcting me. 'Before you f-f-fell asleep.'

'A few hours ago?' I blurted out.

Angel moved swiftly and pressed a finger to my lips. I was about to protest when she pointed towards the corner of the hut. I understood immediately. With everybody in bed, there was nobody sat on the bucket. If we weren't careful, Odd – depending on if he was awake or not – would be able to hear every word we said.

I sat back down on my bed and urged Angel to come closer. 'What's wrong?' I whispered.

'Nothing,' she shrugged. 'Except it's m–m–midnight. Twelve o'clock. You said—'

'Of course I did.' I had forgotten all about going exploring with Priscilla's pass, not that I was about to admit that to Angel. 'How do you know what time it is?' I asked instead.

'I c-c-can't explain it,' Angel began. 'It just comes na–na–naturally.' She stopped and touched my arm. 'Be careful, won't you? I'd h-h-hate for you to end up in Isolation.'

'You're not the only one,' I said, standing up to leave. 'And I won't. Hopefully not, anyway. Keep your fingers crossed.'

'I-I-I will.' Angel followed me as I made my way towards the door. 'I d-d-don't want to stay here forever,' she said sadly. 'I want to go home. And I think you can m-m-make that happen. You're our only hope.'

I turned around and saw that there were tears running down Angel's cheeks. 'Don't ... erm ... do that,' I said, patting her awkwardly on the shoulder. 'You'll make the floor all slippery. I might even fall over.'

'Sorry,' mumbled Angel, wiping her eyes on her boiler suit. 'Don't t-t-tell the others, though. That I'm a Sobber—'

'You're not,' I argued. 'You're a Survivor. Like Mo and Dodge and Wheelie. And me. Don't forget about me. We're a team. We stick together. We survive ... and then we get out of here! Eventually,' I added.

'I'm not as str-str-strong as the rest of you,' stammered Angel.

'You don't have to be,' I insisted. 'You've got other skills. You picked my pockets and stole the pass before Odd could find it. That was amazing. And you stripped that Savage down to his underpants in the blink of an eye. Admittedly, that was kind of weird, but it was still impressive.'

Angel couldn't help but smile. For now at least, I had done enough to comfort her. 'Go back to bed and get some sleep,' I said quietly. 'Don't worry about me. I'll be fine. Sneaking about in the shadows is what I do best.'

'L-L-Like a spy?' said Angel.

'Yeah, something like that.' Turning away from her, I pressed the pass to the control panel by the door until it *clicked*. With the door unlocked, I pushed it open, stepped outside the hut ... and slipped down the ramp, landing flat on my bum at the bottom.

Ouch!

I stood up quickly and brushed myself down. I was okay, albeit a little embarrassed. Still, at least nobody had been there to see me fall. And when I say nobody what I really mean is Angel. That would've been humiliating. Especially after everything I had just said to her.

'Are you o-o-okay?'

I heard the whisper and glanced over my shoulder. Angel was stood in the doorway with her hands up to her mouth. She looked concerned. I gave her a wave to reassure her and she was about to wave back when the door to the hut automatically closed.

I was on my own now.

I stayed low as I peered up at the nearest watchtower to me. The guards were still in place, but I doubted they could see me in the darkness. I started to wonder if they were the same guards as before or if they had changed over at some point. If they had, where did they go when they weren't working? Did they know a way off Odd Island? There had to be one, of course. Odd and Norman had snatched me and all the other children from the streets, so how did they manage to get there and back so easily? As far as I could tell there were no roads in or out of the compound. Or either a runway for an airplane or a landing pad for a helicopter. I hadn't been everywhere, of course, but something of that size would have been practically impossible to hide.

I tapped my head and tried to concentrate. Tonight's little adventure wasn't about escaping; it was about food. With that in mind I followed the searchlights as they swept across the courtyard. It didn't take me long to understand their pattern. Starting at the Nerve Centre, they moved anti-clockwise in a wide arc as they lit up the huts one at a time before eventually returning to the beginning. The whole process took between thirteen and fourteen seconds. Call me awkward, but I settled on thirteen-and-a-half.

Thirteen-and-a-half seconds for me to outrun the lights and make it all the way to the Nerve Centre.

Yes, I could do that.

Definitely.

Maybe.

Maybe not.

I waited with bated breath until the searchlight passed over my head, and then …

Go, Hugo. Go.

It turns out that thirteen-and-a-half seconds goes faster than I had imagined. I had almost reached the Nerve Centre when I felt the heat of the searchlight coming up behind me. I took two more steps and then dived towards the building.

Rolling over, I pressed my body against the bricks as the light passed over my head. Somehow, it missed me. With only a few seconds to spare before it came around again, though, I removed the pass from my pocket and crawled forward.

The light was almost upon me when I waved my hand in front of the control panel.

Nothing happened.

I dropped down out of sight and studied the pass. Not only was it covered in scratches, but there was dirt stuck to one corner. I rubbed it with my finger and then tried to wipe it off on my boiler suit. It didn't look much better once I had finished, but what else could I do? The searchlight passed again and I knew I had another thirteen-and-a-half seconds.

Scrambling to my feet, I got as close to the door as possible before pressing the pass against the panel.

This time it *clicked*.

Yanking on the handle, I rushed inside as quickly and yet as quietly as I could. I was halfway through the door when the searchlight passed for the umpteenth time and illuminated my moving body. I waited for an alarm to sound. One … two … three. I stopped waiting on the fourth second and closed the door gently behind me.

I had done it. I was safely inside the Nerve Centre.

I took a look around as I caught my breath. The corridor was just as I remembered. Long and narrow with a deep, red carpet and numerous doors on either side of me, all of which were closed.

All except one.

The door at the very end of the corridor, the door to Ebenezer Odd's bedroom, was wide open. Not only that, but the light was on and I could hear voices coming from inside. Voices meant people and people meant trouble.

I had assumed everybody would be asleep by now.

Unfortunately, I had assumed wrong.

22.'DON'T MAKE ME TWO.'

It didn't take me long to recognise the voices.

One was the monotonous drone of Ebenezer Odd himself, whilst the other was the high-pitched whine of Priscilla. Also known as Number One. Daddy's favourite.

Although, by the sound of things, not for much longer.

Desperate to get his point across, Odd was still lecturing Priscilla like he had done out in the courtyard earlier on in the evening. With no wish to listen to him all over again, I was about to leave them to it when one word stood out above all the others.

'Twenty ...'

That was my number. My name if you like. They were talking about me.

My head told me to forget about it and concentrate on finding the food instead. The problem is, when have I ever listened to my head? I mean, it's not as if I keep my brains in there, is it? Oh, I do. Seriously? Wow. You learn something new every day, don't you?

Against my better judgment, I crept quietly towards Odd's bedroom. Nobody needed to tell me that this was the wrong thing to do. If either Odd or Priscilla were to look outside at any point, I was doomed. With nowhere to hide, it would be impossible for them not to see me. And then what? I suppose I could always tell Odd that I had found the pass and come to return it. Yes, that would probably work. Odd was sure to fall for that.

Wasn't he?

I knelt down when I reached the entrance and peeked around the door. Odd was resting in his favourite chair, the same one that I had mistakenly sat on the first time we had met. Laid in his lap, purring contentedly, was the cat, Mrs Snuggleflops. I ducked out of sight when I thought she had seen me, before deciding that it didn't really matter if she had. I mean, it's not as if she could tell Odd that I was there. Not with words anyway. Only *meows*. And they don't really count.

'It's not a difficult question,' sighed Odd. 'What do you think of Twenty?'

'The new boy?' Sat cross-legged on the carpet, Priscilla began to furiously shake her head. 'I don't like him, Daddy. Not in the slightest. Not one teeny, tiny bit.'

Okay, there's no need to go on about it. I have got feelings.

'Of course you don't like him,' remarked Odd, as if it was so obvious it didn't need saying. 'But what do you *think* of him? Do you find him … *different* to the others?'

'He's a lot uglier if that's what you mean,' replied Priscilla.

Charming.

'No, it's more than just his face,' continued Odd. 'He's only just arrived and yet he's caused more trouble than all my other children put together. He's at the scene of every crime. He's everywhere he shouldn't be and nowhere he should. He's a problem. And every problem needs a solution.'

'You're right, Daddy,' nodded Priscilla. 'Twenty's to blame for everything.'

'Not everything.' Odd wagged his finger at her. 'You're *definitely* to blame for the missing pass. It was yours to look after and you lost it.'

'I didn't lose it, Daddy,' argued Priscilla. 'It was stolen.'

'So you keep on saying,' Odd groaned. 'But who by? We searched Twenty. He didn't have it anywhere on him.'

'Maybe he hid it,' blurted out Priscilla. 'Or swallowed it. Or made it disappear. Yes, that's it. He could be a magician. We never thought of that, Daddy.'

'There's a reason we never thought of that!' cried Odd. 'It's ridiculous! Mark my words, though. I *will* get to the bottom of the missing pass, but that's not why I've summoned you here. You've let me down and now you must suffer the consequences. You know what I'm going to do, don't you?'

I didn't like the sound of that. Okay, so I'd hardly class Priscilla as a friend, but if Odd started to hurt her in some way then the least I would have to do was try and stop him.

'No, Daddy,' Priscilla pleaded.

'*Yes*, Daddy.' Raising a hand into the air, Odd twirled his forefinger repeatedly before pointing it straight at Priscilla.

'From now on, you will be known by one number and one number only. And that number is … *Two*.'

'Two?' Priscilla squealed. 'No, not Two. Anything but Two. Please …'

'Don't beg! It's undignified,' scowled Odd. 'Besides, my mind is made up. As bad as things may seem right now, there is a way for you to redeem yourself. It won't be enjoyable, but that's the cost of failing me, I'm afraid.'

'What is it?' asked a sulking Priscilla.

'I would like you to spy on Twenty,' began Odd. 'First, you will need to make friends with him—'

'That's not possible,' moaned Priscilla. 'He's a boy. And he smells.'

I screwed up my face. Didn't Priscilla know I could hear every word she said? Oh no, she didn't, did she? I'll let her off then.

'First, you will make friends with him,' repeated Odd. 'You need to gain his confidence so he opens up. Then you can report back to me. Tell me everything he says and does—'

'Everything?' frowned Priscilla.

'*Almost* everything,' insisted Odd. 'I don't want to know how often he picks his nose or scratches his armpit. It's the peculiar stuff I'm interested in. If he's up to anything suspicious then I'm sure you'll find out.' Odd paused. 'Do I make myself clear … Two?'

Priscilla dropped her head. 'Yes, Daddy,' she nodded. 'I'll do as you ask. And then I can be One again?'

'We'll see,' said Odd. 'Twenty's my biggest concern at

the moment. He's a bad egg ... and bad eggs need to be cracked, preferably before they begin to stink. Right, I think that's enough for tonight, Two. Norman will see you out. And then he can fetch me my midnight feast. Isn't that so, my special boy?'

I froze as the big goon appeared from out of the shadows. He had been so still, so quiet, that I hadn't noticed him before. Now, however, I couldn't fail to miss him.

Thankfully, Norman wasn't looking in my direction. With his eyes fixed on a spot on the wall, he marched over to Priscilla and lifted her off the carpet as if he was picking up an empty sweet wrapper. I guessed that his next move would be to leave via the door.

Yes, that's the same door that I was knelt behind.

I scrambled to my feet as both Norman and Priscilla appeared in the doorway. As luck would have it, they were still facing away from me. They had no idea I was there. But that would all change the moment they left the room.

Norman was about to do just that when Priscilla wriggled free of his clutches.

'Please, Daddy,' she begged, diving at Odd's feet. 'I'm One. Your favourite.'

'Prove it then,' said Odd. 'Spy on Twenty and I'll think about reinstating you. As for now, back to your dormitory ... *Two.*'

Priscilla was about to howl out loud when Norman stuck a hand over her mouth before lifting her up with the other. That was my cue to leave. Spinning away from the doorway, it was easy for me to move fast across the carpet without anyone hearing. I didn't have time to remove the pass from my pocket so I grabbed at every door handle instead. The first three I tried were locked.

The fourth, however, wasn't.

I opened it slightly and slipped inside. I thought about closing it behind me before deciding to leave a gap just large enough to peek through. Norman was coming up the corridor with Priscilla over his shoulder. I crossed my fingers that he hadn't seen me. And then uncrossed them when he walked straight past and exited the Nerve Centre.

I took a moment to cast an eye over my surroundings. I was in a bedroom. Well, it was a room with a bed in it. That was close enough. A simple metal frame with a thin mattress and a flat pillow, it was longer than any bed I had ever seen. At a guess it belonged to Norman. There was no other furniture or ornaments in there apart from a framed picture on the wall. It was a photograph of two people, one of whom was Ebenezer Odd. He was at least twenty years younger than he was now, but there was no mistaking the floppy fringe and smug grin. Norman was stood beside him. He was about the same age as me, but that was where any similarities ended. Even then he was huger than huge and towered over Odd with ease. Just like nowadays, his face was set in stone, whilst his eyes stared blankly into the distance. Odd, meanwhile, looked particularly pleased with himself as he pointed up at a sign above his head. The sign said *Oddstoppable Film Studios.*

I was still staring at the picture when I heard a noise outside. I moved quickly towards the door and peeked out into the corridor. It was empty. There was no one in sight.

But that didn't hide the fact that I had wasted too much time in Norman's bedroom.

My senses were on red alert as I continued along the corridor in search of the kitchen. Using the pass, the first room I entered was a store cupboard. There were mops and buckets everywhere I looked, not to mention cloths and sprays and brushes and pans. The second room, meanwhile, was like the world's largest walk-in wardrobe. Nearly all available floor space was filled with row upon row of racks, all of which was packed tight with clothing. My first thought was that it must have belonged to all the children who had been brought to Odd Island. I realised I was wrong when I spotted military uniforms and even a random spacesuit amongst the racks. It didn't make sense. Not unless Buck had arrived dressed as a spaceman.

I left the room and started to wonder how long this was going to take. Not long actually because one door later I struck gold.

Gold being the kitchen.

Larger than the other rooms I had entered, if anything it reminded me of the kind of kitchen you'd find in a restaurant with its stainless steel work tables and industrial-sized ovens. I stumbled upon the fridge without looking, but then it was so big and shiny there was no way I could possibly miss it. Pulling open the door, my mouth fell open. Yes, I had been hoping to find food, but this was beyond my wildest expectations.

Quite simply, the fridge was bursting at the seams. Overstocked and overflowing. Piled high and pressed together. There were so many sweet treats in there, in fact, it was hard to know where to start.

Hard ... but not impossible.

I spun around and snatched a grey sack like the ones Priscilla had used from a work table behind me. With no time to waste, I set about filling it as quickly as possible. I had been worried about taking too much in case anybody noticed, but there was no chance of that. Not with so much food inside.

It didn't take me long to fill the bag. Thankfully, I had nearly finished. Just one more doughnut ...

I was half in, half out of the fridge when the door to the kitchen swung open. Without thinking, I dropped to my knees and crawled backwards until I found myself hidden from view under one of the work tables. As hiding places went it was somewhere in between. Neither good nor bad. I could be seen, yes, but only if you knew where to look.

I listened hard and heard the familiar stomp of heavy footsteps. They got louder and louder before a huge pair of feet wandered into view.

It was Norman.

I assumed he must have been searching for me before my brain stirred and I remembered Odd's last request. He wanted Norman to collect his midnight feast. That was a relief. A *massive* relief. Because for one moment there—

My heart skipped, tripped and flipped a beat when I spotted the grey sack full of food. I had been so keen to hide that I had left it in the middle of the floor. Without thinking, I reached out and dragged it towards me until it was out of sight. Phew. That was another relief, because for one moment there—

No, not again.

The door to the fridge was wide open. That was my fault. I had gotten greedy and forgotten to close it. On this occasion, however, there was no way I could come to my own rescue. My only option was to leave it how it was.

Careless, Hugo. Very, very careless.

23.'SEE NOTHING … HEAR NOTHING … SAY NOTHING.'

Norman stopped at the fridge.

I held my breath and waited for him to make his move. Even without the glasses he so desperately needed, he still must've noticed that the door was wide open. And if he saw the door, he would see the missing food. Wouldn't he? Maybe … maybe not …

I was still holding my breath when Norman shifted slightly to one side. I wondered what he was thinking. That's if he was thinking at all, of course. There was no proof yet that he knew how to do that. Not by himself, anyway.

I almost leapt out of my own skin when Norman broke his own silence.

'See nothing … hear nothing … say nothing,' he muttered. Reaching inside the fridge, he took an entire sponge cake from the top shelf before closing the door behind him.

I tried not to get my hopes up, but the big lump seemed to be leaving. A part of me still believed that it might be a trap, though, and he would pounce on me as soon as I showed myself. I suppose there was only one way to find out ...

I waited until Norman's footsteps had faded before I crawled out from under the work table. Standing up slowly, I kept my head down as I took a look around. I was just in time to see the kitchen door close. Norman had gone. I was sure of it.

And, if I had my way, I wouldn't be far behind him.

I grabbed the grey sack, but it was heavier than I expected so I dragged it across the floor instead. There was definitely enough food in there to go around. Too much probably, but putting any of it back now was a risk I wasn't prepared to take.

I crept up to the door and pressed the pass against the panel. I waited for the inevitable *click* and then gently pulled down on the handle. To my relief, the corridor to the Nerve Centre was empty. Norman was nowhere to be seen.

My heart was pounding as I left the kitchen and made my way towards the exit. I tried desperately not to rush, but my feet had other ideas. They just wanted to get out of there. So badly, in fact, that I failed to spot that one of the doors along the corridor was open.

The door to Norman's bedroom.

I froze like a fish finger in an ice bath when I spotted the man himself stretched out on his bed with his eyes glued to the ceiling. As far as I could tell he hadn't seen me. But even Norman would have to spot someone stood in his doorway eventually.

Wary of making even the slightest of sounds, I barely

lifted my feet as I shuffled slowly across the carpet. I was almost out of view when, not for the first time, Norman took me by surprise.

'See nothing ... hear nothing ... say nothing,' he murmured. He had said that back in the kitchen. I still didn't know what it meant, but now wasn't the time to ask. With Odd's special boy seemingly happy to ignore me, I continued to shuffle along the corridor until I had left his bedroom well and truly behind.

I used the pass to exit the Nerve Centre. Clutching the bag in both hands, I crouched down and waited for the searchlight to pass over me before I set off across the courtyard as fast as my feet would take me. I told myself not to look at the light as it swung around in an arc above my head. I had thirteen seconds to get to the hut and nothing was going to change that. No, my mistake. I had thirteen-and-a-half. And in the end that extra half-a-second was priceless as I scrambled up the ramp just before the light drew level with me.

The others all seemed to be fast asleep. It was only then that I realised how exhausted I was. Maybe the food could wait until tomorrow.

It was Dodge, however, who woke up a second later and changed my mind.

'Is that you, matey?' he whispered.

I didn't reply. Not at first. Instead, I laid the bag on my bed and emptied the contents across the blanket. Yes, some of it was a little squashed, but it still looked better than anything Odd had ever given us.

'Yes, it's me,' I said, mindful to sit on the bucket before I spoke. 'I'm back. And I've got something to show you.'

Wheelie was the second Survivor to stir. 'Give me a clue. It's not a verruca on your big toe, is it? Or a wart on your nose?'

'Of course not,' I groaned. 'This is more edible than medical.'

It took him a while, but Wheelie eventually sat up and glanced over at my bed.

'Oh … my … whirlwind!' he blurted out. 'Is this a dream? Tell me it's not. Wake up, you lot. You're not going to believe this.'

'Believe what?' mumbled Mo.

'Believe what I'm looking at,' gasped Wheelie. 'It's a—'

'Cream cake,' said Mo, lifting her head from her pillow.

'Cookie,' said Dodge, jumping to his feet.

'No, a doughnut,' argued Wheelie. 'I was looking at a doughnut.'

'And now you're about to eat one,' I said, gesturing towards the food. 'Tuck in, guys. We don't want to leave anything behind. Not even a crumb.'

Unsurprisingly, Wheelie, Dodge and Mo didn't need telling twice. Angel, however, climbed slowly out of bed and tiptoed over to where I was sat.

'I'm p-p-pleased you're back,' she said, placing a hand on my arm.

'You're pleased I'm back with all that food,' I added, smiling up at her.

'The food is j-j-just a bonus,' Angel insisted. 'It's y-y-you we really need.'

'And I need you, too,' I remarked. '*All* of you. I've got some big plans, Angel, and I can't put them into practice without the rest of you Survivors here to help me. Now, do me a favour and pass me a custard slice before my stomach rumbles so loudly that even Odd can hear it!'

I watched as Angel wandered over to my bed without another word, but then shifted my attention to the others as they furiously filled their faces. They looked so happy as they ate. Okay, so stealing is nothing to be proud of, but stealing to survive from someone as vile as Ebenezer Odd was hardly the worst crime ever committed.

Dodge used a chocolate eclair to point at me. 'This is amazing,' he said, grinning from ear to ear. 'You're the best, matey.'

I smiled back at him. There was no denying it; my plan had worked to perfection. I had only been here for a day or so, but it was a good start. That was all it was, though.

A start.

Now it was time to look towards the finish … and that meant escaping from Odd Island!

24. 'YOU'D MAKE A GOOD SPY.'

My stomach was still hurting when the alarm went off.

Yes, you don't have to rub it in. I know I had eaten far too much and that was my own fault. The thing is, I thought I would've had longer to sleep it off. But I was wrong. I only had a few hours. Three at most. And that's not long enough for anybody to sleep off four chocolate brownies, three custard slices, two iced buns and one uncomfortably large sponge cake. Oh, and a banana. Don't forget about the banana. Even spies need to eat their fair share of fruit and veg to stay healthy.

Back in the hut and I had never heard this particular alarm before and had no wish to hear it again. It was so ear-splittingly loud that all five of us had little choice but to sit up and take notice.

'What time is it?' shouted Mo. 'It can't be seven o'clock already.'

'It's f-f-five,' replied Angel, barely audible above the horrible *squeal*.

I was about to ask why we had been woken up two hours early when the door to the hut *clicked* and in stomped

Norman. 'Come,' he said gruffly.

The others climbed out of bed and hurried towards the door on his command. I, meanwhile, went to fetch Wheelie's wheelchair. 'This is exciting,' I muttered to no one in particular. 'I wonder where we're going. Somewhere nice, I hope. I mean, anywhere other than Odd Island would be a start.'

'Courtyard,' grunted Norman. 'Now.'

'No, not the courtyard,' I moaned. 'What a let down! Can't you have a word with darling Daddy and take us somewhere better? You are his special boy, after all.'

Wheelie pulled a face as he climbed into the chair. Not only could he tell that I was being deliberately difficult, but he was trying to warn me against it.

'Courtyard,' repeated Norman. 'Now!'

'Hold your horses,' I grumbled. 'I'm not that great in the morning. Or the afternoon if I'm being honest. And don't even mention the evening! Besides, you've not told me what day it is yet? Tuesday? No, Wednesday? Right, I should probably have told you earlier, but Wednesdays always have a strange effect on me. They call it the middle of the week muddle. It makes me very awkward. And annoying. And argumentative. You know, all the things that can really get on someone's nerves … whoa!'

Norman stepped forward and lunged at me. Fortunately, I saw him coming and swerved swiftly to one side. It left the big lump slightly off-balance so I hopped over Wheelie's bed and followed the others through the door before he had a chance to try again.

It was still dark outside. Not cold though, which surprised me. If it wasn't a frosty start, where were the clouds in the sky? Or the wind? Or the birds? And why was it always so eerily quiet on Odd Island?

I was still waiting for an answer to all those questions (not to mention ninety-seven others that were floating around my head) when Norman came up behind me and pushed me in the back, sending me stumbling down the ramp.

'Sit down, Twenty,' ordered Odd. 'This is important.'

Dressed in a fluffy white dressing gown with even fluffier slippers, he was stood in the middle of the courtyard with the rest of the children all sat around him in a circle. The Suck-ups – led by Priscilla – were as close to Odd as they could possibly get, whilst the Sobbers were already sniffing and snuffling into their hands before Odd had even said a word. Only the Savages seemed pleased to see me … or maybe they were just smiling because I had almost fallen over when Norman had barged into me.

I had barely sat down when Odd drew a breath and got straight to the point.

'We have a thief,' he announced.

Oh. The reason for our early morning wake-up call was starting to take shape.

'The Nerve Centre has been penetrated,' continued Odd. 'One of you, no doubt with the aid of Priscilla's missing pass, gained access to the kitchen and stole a large amount of food. That food, however, was supposed to be shared out amongst you all.'

I fought hard not to burst out laughing. That was a lie.

Odd would've kept that food for himself. There was no way he would've shared it. Not even with Norman.

'I hope the thief is listening because I will make this very simple for them,' said Odd, looking around the circle. 'Own up now and we can all get back to having a lovely day. Yes, you will be punished, but it will be nowhere near as harsh as it could be. If you do not own up, however, the punishment will apply to all of you. No one will escape my wrath.'

With that, the Sobbers burst into tears, whilst the Suck-ups simply gasped in horror.

'The punishment will not be pleasant,' remarked Odd, rubbing his hands together a little too enthusiastically for my liking. 'I have no wish for things to go that far, but what choice do I have? I am an innocent victim in all of this. As are nineteen of my children. There is one, however, who insists on ruining things for everybody.'

The crying was getting worse. I sat up a little and Dodge placed a hand on my arm. I glanced over at him and he gently shook his head.

'This is all becoming so very tedious,' sighed Odd. 'What are you? A spineless specimen? A cowardly custard? Do you enjoy seeing other people suffer because of your actions, you horrible, horrible child?'

My blood was boiling now. I was about to jump up when I felt a much firmer hand on my shoulder, preventing me from doing so. This time it belonged to Mo.

'Have it your way,' sighed Odd. 'If I can't punish one then I shall punish you all. There will be no breakfast and your chores shall start this very minute. Get to work, my children. It will be a long, hard day, I'm afraid.'

Odd was already on his way when I blurted something out by accident. 'Is that all?'

'I beg your pardon, Twenty?' Odd turned on me in a flash. 'Is my punishment not harsh enough for you?'

'No,' I replied, climbing to my feet. 'Or is it yes? Who knows? Not me, that's for certain. To tell you the truth I'm not entirely sure I even understand the question.'

'Maybe you'd prefer to spend a day or two in Isolation,' remarked Odd, trying not to smile. 'You could join Zero. You have heard of Zero, haven't you? He had a number once. Then he had it removed.'

'Oh, I bet he was in tears about that,' I muttered. 'What did he do that was so bad?'

'Zero tried to leave,' revealed Odd. 'Tried … and failed. And now he's paying the price for his actions.'

'Did he get far?' I asked, perking up a little.

'Far enough,' replied Odd. By the look on his face, though, he had said something he regretted. 'You do not ask me questions, Twenty,' he hissed. 'Zero let himself down and now he serves as a warning to all of you. Be happy here. Enjoy your time on Odd Island. Because if you don't, if you dare to cross the line, then you will be banished … forever!'

Odd was raging now. I wondered what he was going to do next when Wheelie appeared between us.

'Isolation isn't the answer,' he insisted. At the same time he handed me a sweeping brush. 'We'll just get on with our chores and be grateful for what we have. You called Odd Island the loveliest place known to mankind when I first arrived, Daddy, and that's how I want it to stay. I'm sure you feel the same way, don't you, Twenty?'

I screwed up my face. 'If you say so, Wheel … I mean … Twelve.'

'Thirteen,' said Wheelie, correcting me.

'That's right,' I nodded. 'I was just testing you. And you passed. Congratulations, Four … no, Thirteen.'

Odd had heard enough. Snorting loudly, he spun around on his slippers and headed back towards the Nerve Centre. I grinned at Wheelie and then shuffled over to the fence at the edge of the compound. I had barely started sweeping, however, when I heard movement behind me. I assumed it was Wheelie. Or even Norman.

But I assumed wrong.

'Lovely morning, isn't it?'

I looked over my shoulder and saw Priscilla stood too close for comfort. 'You'd make a good spy, sneaking up on people like that,' I said.

'Spy? Me? No, never,' mumbled Priscilla awkwardly. 'It's Twenty, isn't it?'

'What is?' I asked, confused.

'Your name, silly,' laughed Priscilla. 'You're Twenty.'

'And you're Two,' I replied. The horrified look on Priscilla's face seemed to suggest that she wasn't expecting anyone to know that. 'Word spreads quick around here,' I added. 'I hope you're not too upset.'

'It won't be for long,' snapped Priscilla. She was visibly shaking now. Just for a moment I thought she might blow her top, but somehow she held it together. 'I don't think we got off to the best of starts yesterday,' she said through gritted teeth. 'That was probably down to me—'

'No probably about it,' I muttered.

'But that doesn't mean we can't try again,' insisted Priscilla. 'I'm actually quite nice when you get to know me. Maybe we could even be—'

'Friends?' I said, beating her to it. 'You want us to be friends. Wow. That's some turnaround. Yesterday you did nothing but insult me.'

'No, I didn't,' argued Priscilla. 'Well …maybe I did … just a little … but that was my mistake. Now I've had a good think about things, I'd like us to be friends.'

I pretended to weigh up her offer. 'Yeah, okay,' I nodded eventually. 'We can be friends. Best friends even. Hey, maybe I could move into your hut … we could spend every minute together … never leave each other's sides … from now until the day we leave.'

'Maybe we should take it one step at a time,' said Priscilla hastily. 'We can start by talking more. You can tell me anything you want. Anything you're thinking. Anything you might be … planning.'

'Great,' I said, grinning at her. 'I'll tell you everything. Every last detail. I can even tell you how many times I pick my nose or scratch my armpits.'

Priscilla's eyes began to narrow. She knew that something wasn't right, but she couldn't quite put her finger on what it was.

'Farewell, my new friend.' Grabbing Priscilla by the shoulders, I spun her round and pushed her in the right direction. 'I can't wait for us to speak again,' I said. 'And don't worry about our little secret. My lips are sealed.'

'What secret?' asked Priscilla nervously.

'Your number,' I explained. 'You don't like it, do you … Two? But I won't tell anyone … Two. Not if you don't want me to … Two. You can trust me … Two.'

I waved at Priscilla as she finally walked away. As far as she was concerned, she had done exactly what Odd had demanded of her.

And yet none of it was true.

We weren't really friends and there was no way I'd be telling her a thing.

Priscilla didn't know it, but I had her exactly where I wanted her. What's that old saying? Never look a gift shop in the letterbox. No, not that one. Keep your friends close and your enemies closer. Yes, that's it. Priscilla may have just walked away, but she was actually closer than ever.

'What did she want?' asked Wheelie, joining me by the fence.

'To make friends,' I replied.

'To make friends?' Wheelie's mouth fell open. 'With you?'

'I'm not that bad,' I muttered.

'You know what I mean,' frowned Wheelie. 'Priscilla made it perfectly clear yesterday that she doesn't like you. She doesn't like any of us. So, what's changed?'

'Her number, that's what.' I could tell by Wheelie's face that he was more confused than ever. 'Let me explain—'

'There's no time,' said Wheelie, interrupting me. 'Don't

look now, but we've got company.'

I looked. Obviously. The company in question was Norman. He was striding across the courtyard, determined to split us up. For once I didn't mind, though. I had a plan, but I hadn't quite perfected it yet.

Yes, another plan. There's not a set limit. I can have as many as I like. This particular one had come to me when Odd had told me about Zero and what he had attempted. All of a sudden there was somewhere I wanted to go. Somewhere I could hopefully find some answers. Pick up some clues. Maybe even unearth some truths about Odd Island.

Somewhere like … Isolation.

25.'GIVE ME THAT CAT!'

'You're going to kidnap Mrs Snuggleflops?'

That was Wheelie. It was funny, but the way he said it made it sound like a bad idea. And it wasn't. It was great. Inspired even. But that was largely because it was me who had come up with it.

'Yes, that's exactly what I'm going to do,' I replied. It was lunchtime and I was sat on my bed with a bowl of ... give me a second to check ... soup. I couldn't be certain, but I think I was supposed to be eating it. That wasn't going to happen, though. No way whatsoever. 'Although, just to be accurate,' I continued, 'Mrs Snuggleflops isn't actually a kid, is she? She's a cat. So maybe I'll just ... um ... *catnap* her.'

'A catnap's a lot different than a kidnap, you melon,' groaned Mo.

'No, you're thinking of a cat *flap*,' remarked Dodge, waving his spoon at her. 'That's nothing like a catnap ... or a mousetrap ... or a—'

'Handicap,' added Wheelie. 'That's my specialist subject. I thought it best I say it before anyone else does. Right, what were we talking about again?'

'Hugo's going to *cat kidnap* Mrs Snuggleflops,' sighed Mo, shaking her head in disbelief.

'Not forever,' I insisted. 'Once Odd has found her he can have her back. That shouldn't take long.'

'He'll go bonkers, matey,' cried Dodge. 'If you're not careful you'll end up in Isolation.'

'Yeah, that's the idea,' I grinned.

'This is getting crazier by the second,' grumbled Mo. 'You *want* to go to Isolation.'

'Only for a day,' I insisted. 'I'm not completely crackers. But I am desperate. We all are. If we're going to get off Odd Island then I need to speak to Zero. None of you have ever seen him before so he must've been holed up in Isolation for ages. Weeks probably. For Odd to leave him there that long makes me think he must've got quite far when he tried to escape. Nearly all the way perhaps. And if I can find out how he did it then maybe we can go one better.'

The hut fell silent.

'It's risky,' said Dodge eventually. 'Get stuck in Isolation and you might never come out.'

'That's not going to happen,' I shrugged.

'You don't know that,' argued Mo.

'Yes, I do,' I said firmly. I didn't, of course. How could I? Mo was glaring at me so I switched my gaze to someone else. Someone not quite so intimidating. 'What do you reckon, Angel?' I asked. 'Do you think it's a good plan?'

Angel was sat on the bucket in the corner of the room. Not the best place to eat your soup (but then no place was ideal when it came to eating that slop).

'I-I-I like it,' she replied, looking up. 'It might not w-w-work, but I like it.'

'I knew you would,' I said, winking at her. 'If only the others weren't quite so negative—'

'Oh, just do what you want,' said Mo gruffly. 'You always do anyway. One question, though. When are you planning on snatching Odd's favourite four-legged friend and how are you going to do it?'

'Well, it's funny you should ask me that …' Without another word, I reached under my bed and removed something small and fluffy. 'I saw her hanging around the courtyard and thought she looked lonely,' I said, placing the cat on my pillow. 'Say hello to Mrs Snuggleflops everybody, the cutest little fur-ball on the whole of Odd Island.'

'Hello, Mrs Sn-Sn-Snuggleflops,' said Angel.

'This is going to end badly, matey,' frowned Dodge.

'That's true,' I nodded. 'You four don't want to get caught up in this if you can help it. If I was you I'd leave before the—' I was cut off by the shrill squall of a shrieking siren. 'Alarm goes off,' I shouted, finishing my own sentence. I quickly ushered them towards the door. 'Go. I'll see you soon. I promise.'

They did as I asked and hurried out into the courtyard. At the same time I sat down on my bed and picked up Mrs Snuggleflops. 'You don't think Daddy will be too mad, do you?'

She didn't answer. Bit rude. I was about to ask her again when Norman burst into the hut. As expected, Odd was right behind him.

'I might have known,' he hissed at me. 'You've … stolen … my … cat!'

'Not stolen … borrowed,' I insisted. 'There's a big difference. I found her in the courtyard in case you're wondering. She seemed distressed so I came to her rescue. Hey, some people might even call me a hero—'

'Give me that cat!' A furious Odd charged towards me and snatched Mrs Snuggleflops out of my hands. 'After everything we spoke about this morning and you still dare to cross me,' he scowled. 'Your behaviour is unacceptable, Twenty. This time your punishment will be both swift and severe.'

'Yeah, that sounds about right to me,' I said, nodding in agreement.

Odd lifted his child zapper in anger.

'Whoa!' I said hastily. 'That's severe, but is it really severe enough.'

'No, you're right,' said Odd, lowering his weapon before he glanced over at Norman.

'Not *him* again,' I sighed. 'No offence to your special boy, but we're getting really rather bored of one another. You know what it's like. If someone pokes and pushes and shoves and spins and dumps and drops you all day everyday then it does tend to get a little bit … samey-samey after a while.'

'I know what you need,' cried Odd, rubbing his hands together with glee. 'A week in Isolation.'

'A week?' I repeated. 'Bit much. I only borrowed your cat …'

'Stole,' argued Odd. 'You do make a good point, though. Three days in Isolation ...'

'Getting closer,' I said, 'but I still don't think I've done anything that bad—'

'Silence, Twenty!' spat Odd. 'I have made up my mind. You will spend one day in Isolation and that is final. One day for you to learn from your mistakes. When you come out you will be a changed boy. Unrecognisable from the beastly brat who stands before me now.'

'Perfect,' I said, leaping up off the bed. 'I'm ready when you are. Or would you prefer it if I led the way ...'

I set off towards the exit, but didn't get far before a cover was thrown over my head and I was plunged into darkness. Next thing I knew I was being hoisted into the air and tossed over a shoulder. Norman's at a guess. There was no way that Odd could carry me with such ease.

I bounced up and down with his footsteps as we made our way down the ramp and across the courtyard. We hadn't gone far, however, before Norman came to a sudden halt and dropped me without warning. It wasn't the softest of landings, but that wasn't what concerned me. Somewhat foolishly perhaps, I had assumed that Isolation would be one of the many closed off-rooms inside the Nerve Centre. We hadn't walked that far, though, and this certainly wasn't carpet I had landed on.

The cover was removed from my head. I was in some kind of hole. It was big enough to sit up in, but you could barely stretch your legs. Worse than that, however, there was nobody else in there.

Where was Zero?

I looked up and saw Norman looming over me. He was holding a huge piece of wood above his head. Like a lid. And everybody knows what you do with a lid. You use it to cover something.

Or, in this case, someone.

'Wait!' I blurted out. 'There must be a mistake.'

'No mistake.' With that, Norman crouched down and lowered the wood on top of me, plunging me into darkness. I pushed against it, but he had already secured it in place.

I was trapped.

It was a tiny space, but that didn't mean I had to panic. Shifting slightly to one side, I tried to get comfortable, but found that my knees were pressed under my nostrils and my head rubbed against the lid.

'Norman ... please,' I shouted. 'You need to get me out of here.'

'He can't hear you.'

The voice was over to my right, somewhere beyond the solid wall of concrete beside me.

'Hello,' I called out. 'Where are you?'

'Next door.' The voice was muffled, but if I pressed my ear to the wall I could just about make out everything that was being said. 'This is the first time I've had a neighbour. You must've done something really bad to end up in Isolation.'

'I've done worse,' I admitted. 'You must be Zero.'

'Is that what they call me?' the voice sighed. 'I'm not even a number.'

'No, you're better than that,' I said. 'You're one of a kind. You almost did the unthinkable. Almost … but not quite. And that's why I had to come and see you.' I stopped to snatch a breath. 'I'm going to succeed where you failed,' I declared. 'I'm going to escape from Odd Island … and you're going to help me do it!'

26.'BE CAREFUL WHAT YOU WISH FOR ...'

.

Zero fell silent.

'You are still there, aren't you?' I asked.

More silence.

'Don't tell me you've fallen asleep,' I moaned. 'I mean, I know I'm boring from time to time, but that's just rude.'

Still more silence.

'Oh, come on,' I cried. 'I only said I wanted to escape. Nothing too crazy.'

'There is no escape from Odd Island,' remarked Zero. 'It's impossible. End of conversation.'

Ah, that was better. At least he was talking now. Even if it wasn't quite the message I wanted to hear.

'Well, you would say that, wouldn't you?' I argued. 'I don't mean to be rude, but you failed. I'm not you, though. I'm ... um ... different.'

'Different?' snorted Zero. 'You are not so different from me. I, too, thought there was a better life out there. I was wrong ...'

Now it was my turn to fall silent. The way Zero spoke was starting to worry me. Not just what he said, but the way he said it. His voice was deeper than any child I had ever met. So much so, in fact, that he could easily have been a fully grown man.

'You think the grass is greener ...' Zero continued.

'The grass doesn't really concern me,' I admitted. 'But, now you mention it, why is there no grass on Odd Island?'

'Spoilt ... self-centred ... ungrateful ...' Zero was ranting and raving now. 'You don't appreciate the things you have here.'

'What? Like mouldy bread, lumpy soup and a bed as hard as Norman's fist?' I grumbled. 'Yeah, you're right. Sometimes I don't realise how lucky I am.'

'Selfish,' remarked Zero.

'Not as far as I can remember,' I replied. 'I don't think we've had any kind of fish—'

'You talk, but you don't listen,' Zero shot back. 'Ebenezer Odd has given you a home.'

'I've already got a home,' I argued. 'It's ... um ... back home. Yes, it's a little shabby around the edges and, yes, my parents can be quite annoying at times – not to mention a *lot* annoying all the other times in between – but it's where I live. I've even got a shedroom. I can come and go as I please. This, however ... this is more like a prison!'

'Freedom is overrated,' muttered Zero.

His words were ringing alarm bells now. He might have tried to escape from Odd Island in the past, but now he was doing everything he could to defend it.

'How old are you?' I asked. 'It's just … your voice … it's very deep. You know, like a polar bear blowing on a trombone.'

'My age, like the passing of time, is no longer of concern to me,' replied Zero. 'Days turn to night and night turns to day, but the darkness never ceases. I'm not complaining, though. Daddy keeps me here for my own safety. I realise that now. He fears that if he lets me out I will try and do something foolish again. Like escape.'

'And would you?' I asked.

'Never,' said Zero firmly. 'Daddy has shown me the error of my ways. I've learnt my lesson. I've changed.'

I screwed up my face. Trapped with only his own thoughts for company, Zero had somehow been brainwashed into thinking only good things about the man who had stuck him in Isolation to begin with. Trying to make him see sense now, after all this time, was like banging my head against a brick wall. Both painfully pointless and pointlessly painful.

'I'm not going to argue with you,' I began, 'but I would like to know how you almost got off the island. Is there a hole in the fence? Or some way over it perhaps? What about a key? A secret tunnel? Or a—?'

'Enough,' said Zero. 'You're wasting your time. Yours *and* mine.'

'Please,' I begged. 'What did you do? You must've got close for Odd to keep you locked up for so long.'

'Daddy is only trying to protect me,' Zero insisted. 'He protects us all. Keeps us safe.'

'Safe from who? There's nobody else here!' The whole

165

thing was so frustrating that I started to laugh. 'Daddy's completely lost the plot. He's stark-raving mad—'

'Don't say that!' The change in Zero's voice was so remarkable that I almost banged my head against the wall. For some reason he had switched from unnaturally deep to ridiculously high-pitched in a single sentence. Squeaky even. And more than vaguely familiar.

There was only one person who sounded like that on Odd Island. And now I had angered him so much that he had given himself away.

'I am not a role model,' said Zero eventually. 'I did something wrong and now I am being punished. That is all I have to say. Heed my warning though, Twenty. Be careful what you wish for ...'

And that was that. Zero wouldn't speak again. I was sure of it. Not that I wanted him to. Unfortunately, it left me in a particularly sticky situation.

Sticky as in stuck.

Stuck in Isolation.

Yes, I know I asked for it, but as things stood I ran the risk of running out of air. Or dying of starvation. Still, at least I had my toenails to nibble on.

Think, Hugo, think.

No, I had nothing. Less than that, in fact. My mind was blanker than blank. Still, at least I knew how Norman felt each and every single day.

Think harder.

I strained my brain until my cheeks turned red. That was when I realised I wasn't thinking at all. No, I was just holding my breath. Which, all things considered, wasn't the cleverest thing to do in a hole as small as this one.

Gasping for air, I was about to call out when the lid was suddenly lifted and a cover was thrown over my head. Before I knew it I had been hauled out of the hole and slung over a shoulder. We were back on the move. And then, just like that, we weren't.

Not for the first time that day I was dropped from a height. And not for the first time it wasn't the softest of landings.

I was still aching, in fact, when the cover was removed from my head.

'Did you miss me?' I groaned.

'Not in the slightest,' replied Mo.

I pushed myself up and waited for my eyes to adjust to the light. I was on the floor of the hut, surrounded by the other Survivors.

'Take this,' said Wheelie, handing me one of his crutches. 'By the look of things you're going to need it.'

I grabbed it with both hands and tried to stand. 'What day is it?' I asked.

'Calm down, matey,' laughed Dodge. 'You've only been gone a few minutes.'

'Tw-Tw-Twenty-three to be precise.' I turned to see Angel stood behind me. As usual, she looked more concerned about my safety than anybody else. And that even included me. 'I-I-I was keeping count,' she added.

Mo wandered over to the bucket and sat down so we were safe to speak. 'So, where have you been for the past twenty-three minutes? Surely not Isolation …'

'Surely *yes* Isolation,' I said, correcting her. 'Turns out it was only a fleeting visit. Still, I suppose Odd had to do something to stop you lot begging for me to be released—'

'Stop waffling and get to the point,' said Wheelie bluntly. 'Did you meet Zero?'

I drew a breath. 'No, I didn't … because Zero doesn't exist.'

'Zero doesn't exist?' Dodge's jaw dropped so much I could see straight down his throat. 'No, that can't be true. I thought—'

'*We* all thought,' I said, butting in. 'We all thought because we were all told. Told by the same person. Let's call him the storyteller. Because that's what he does. He tells us stories and we all believe them.'

'I d-d-don't understand,' frowned Angel.

'No, neither do I,' I admitted. 'But there is one thing I'm certain of. I may not have met Zero in Isolation, but I did meet someone.'

'Tell us, matey,' said Dodge, urging me on. 'Who was it?'

'I met the storyteller,' I replied, nodding at everyone in turn. 'I met Ebenezer Odd.'

27.'THE OUTSIDE WORLD IS WAITING FOR YOU.'

I had figured it out in Isolation.

It was the way he spoke that gave him away. No child ever talked like that. Not even many adults. Only oddballs who were putting on a voice. And I knew one oddball in particular who would definitely try to fool me given the chance. He may even have gotten away with it if he hadn't got so angry. Oh, and he had called me Twenty.

I had never told Zero my number.

Ebenezer Odd, however, could hardly forget it.

He probably thought he could brainwash me by separating me from the others, but he was wrong. He had tried to put me off escaping, but it had only made me more determined. The same problem, though, still remained.

I had no idea how to do it.

Zero was supposed to have filled in the gaps, but, instead, the gaps had just got wider. And the biggest of those gaps stretched all the way from Odd Island to Crooked Elbow.

To Everyday Avenue.

To home.

How could I get from A to B when A refused to let me leave?

Unusually for me, I spent the afternoon with my head down and my mouth shut as I pushed the sweeping brush around the compound. Priscilla had tried to speak to me on several occasions, but I hadn't paid her much attention. She could spy on me all she liked. She wouldn't find anything out. Nothing interesting, anyway. Nothing that Odd could hold against me.

Talking of Odd, I couldn't be certain, but he seemed to be watching me at every turn. What he couldn't see, however, was my brain. That was working overtime.

There had to be a way to get off Odd Island. So, what was it?

It was dark by the time we stopped for the day. My legs were aching and my back felt ready to snap. Worse than that, I had drawn a blank when it came to escape routes.

The buzz of the previous night's adventures had most certainly worn off as the five of us trudged back to the hut and collapsed onto our beds. Dinner was fast approaching, but it was nothing to look forward to. Unlike last night, there were no stolen treats to enjoy. No cakes or cookies. Not even any fruit. Yes, I still had Priscilla's pass, but I couldn't risk using it. It was too soon for that. Maybe tomorrow if I was feeling brave.

'You're v-v-very quiet.'

I jumped at the sight of Angel crouched down beside my bed.

'It's been a long day, that's all,' I said. 'I'm tired.'

Angel rested a hand on my arm. 'Don't lose hope. You never know when an op-op-opportunity might present itself.'

I was about to reply when the door flew open and someone beat me to it.

It was Norman.

'Out!' he ordered.

I guessed he was talking to me, even if he was looking at a spot somewhere above my head.

'Nice to see you, too,' I said, sitting up. 'How have you been? I've missed you. But then who wouldn't? You're a real chatterbox ... whoa!'

Norman moved quickly and dragged me off the bed. 'Out!'

I picked myself up and followed the others outside. The rest of the children were already waiting. The Suck-ups. The Sobbers. And the Savages. As usual, they were sat in a circle. This time, however, they were over to one side of the courtyard, closer to the electric fence. My old friend (not true) Buck glared at me as I wandered down the ramp so I gave him a little wave. The glare only intensified which I took as a victory.

'Hurry, my children,' said Odd, clapping his hands together. As I'd come to expect, he was stood in the centre of the circle. Mrs Snuggleflops, meanwhile, was nowhere to be seen. 'Sit down and we can begin,' Odd declared.

Like the others, I did as he asked without question. Why was that? Was it just easier? Or was I heading the same way as everybody else?

Had I, Hugo Dare, Agent Minus Thirty-Five, finally given up?

'This is Odd Island,' began Odd, gesturing around wildly with his child zapper. 'A safe haven. An oasis of calm in a world of chaos. More importantly perhaps, it is a home. Our home. For all of us to find peace.' Odd stopped without warning and put a hand to his heart. 'Some, however, see things differently,' he said sadly. 'They think of Odd Island as a prison. How dare they! You are not here as punishment – it is a privilege. I want nothing more than to protect you. And yet, because of one individual, one ungrateful urchin, one selfish specimen, it seems that I have failed.' Odd slowly shook his head. 'One of you wishes to leave,' he said eventually. 'Stand up, Twenty. The time has arrived.'

Whoa! I wasn't expecting that. Truth is, I had drifted off a few minutes ago. No, not asleep. Just resting my eyelids. Now, however, I was wide awake. Had he really just said my number? I stayed where I was and peered around the circle. Everybody was staring at me. I was the centre of attention.

'Stand up, Twenty,' repeated Odd. 'Don't be shy. You're not normally.'

I reluctantly did as he asked and climbed slowly to my feet.

'It's Twenty that doesn't want to be here,' announced Odd. 'Yes, I, too, find it impossible to believe, but it's true. He doesn't like it on Odd Island. And he doesn't like me. Or Norman. Or any of you, come to that. He thinks he's better than us—'

'No, I don't,' I argued.

'Silence,' spat Odd. 'You've said enough already. Besides, your actions speak louder than words. Ever since you've been here you've done nothing but cause mischief. Well, this is where the mischief ends. If you don't want to be here then we don't want you here either. Just leave. It's not as if you'll be missed. I've already … stumbled upon your replacement. A sweet, sweet soul, I found her wandering the streets of Crooked Elbow, lost and confused. She was looking for guidance. And I shall give it to her. You, however, had your chance and blew it. That is why I won't stand in your way, Twenty. In fact, I'll make things easy for you …'

I watched as Norman marched over to the edge of the compound and placed his hands between the grilles of the fence.

'We've turned off the electric current in case you're wondering,' revealed Odd. 'It's completely safe. And now it's completely … open.'

Norman stepped to one side and I spotted it for the very first time. A small door. Built into one of the sections of the fence, it was practically impossible to see unless you knew it was there.

'What's the matter, Twenty?' asked Odd. 'This is what you wanted. The outside world is waiting for you.'

I refused to shift. My escape route may have been staring me straight in the face, but I tried not to look at it.

'Oh, you're not so sure anymore,' said Odd, smirking at me. 'Maybe you'd rather not go out there alone. Does anybody else fancy their chances on Odd Island? In the fog? With the wolves? Does anybody else think they can survive without me? Anybody …?'

I followed Odd's gaze as he looked around the circle. Every last child was sat with their heads down, trying desperately to avoid eye contact.

'Just as I thought,' said Odd smugly. 'My other children aren't as silly as you, Twenty. They know what they've got and they don't want to lose it.'

I held my ground, unsure of my next move.

'What are you waiting for?' laughed Odd. 'Don't tell me you're scared.'

I wasn't. Scared, I mean. Not in the slightest. I was just confused. I couldn't understand why Odd was doing this. It made no sense. Surely the last thing he wanted was for any of us to leave. Even someone as irritating as me.

'This nonsense ends now,' said Odd, to my surprise. 'You've embarrassed yourself enough, Twenty. Now let this be a lesson to you and sit down—'

'No!' With that, I started to walk towards the fence. 'You can't tell me what to do.'

Odd watched me all the way. 'Where are you going?'

'Where do you think?' I replied gruffly. 'Thanks for having me, Ebenezer Odd. Don't worry about following me to the door. I can see myself out …'

28.'THIS IS NOT A CELEBRATION.'

I puffed out my chest and walked briskly through the opening in the fence.

'You're braver than I expected,' remarked Odd. 'Brave ... or just brainless. I can't quite decide which. Either way, this is it. If you leave now, there's no coming back.'

'You make that sound like a bad thing,' I muttered.

I flinched as Norman closed the secret door behind me. I had been searching for a way off the compound and here it was, staring me straight in the face. Now, however, I wasn't so sure.

'Good luck, matey,' Dodge called out. 'You can do this.'

'Silence in the courtyard!' spat Odd. 'The boy is an outsider now. He is not to be encouraged.'

'Keep going,' yelled Wheelie.

'Just don't do anything stupid,' warned Mo. 'At least, not as stupid as usual.'

'Half as stupid should be fine,' added Wheelie.

'I won't tell you again,' screamed Odd, waving his hands about. 'He's no longer one of us. He's a boy without a number.'

'B-B-Believe in yourself.' It was less a shout and more of a whisper, but Angel was trying her best. 'I know I-I-I do.'

It was only then that something peculiar happened. One by one, the children began to clap their hands and stamp their feet. They might not have been by my side, but they were right behind me, cheering me on.

'Stop that!' yelled a furious Odd. 'I won't stand for such noise.'

'You should sit down then,' laughed Wheelie. 'Get yourself a wheelchair. They're very comfortable.'

'Back to your huts,' ordered Odd, jabbing a finger at each and every child. 'This is not a celebration. This is the end.'

And that was my cue to run. I figured I had about one minute to escape. One minute before Odd changed his mind and sent Norman to come and get me. One minute starting from now.

Sixty ... fifty-nine ... fifty-eight ...

I quickly picked up the pace. Wheelie had told me there was a forest out there so that was what I aimed for. I hoped the trees would provide some kind of cover and maybe they would have. Unfortunately, there seemed to be something preventing me from ever reaching them.

And that *something* was fog.

The thickest, densest, most *foggiest* fog I had ever encountered.

Let's just pause for a moment. Does any of this sound familiar? Because it should do. Especially if you've been paying attention. What's that? You haven't? Okay, fair enough. I won't hold it against you. But I will take a second to get you back on track. I actually wrote this way, way back in the prologue. You know, that little bit at the beginning. Just a few pages before chapter one. Oh, you remember now. Well done. You should probably give yourself a pat on the back. Not too hard, of course. I wouldn't want your teeth to fall out.

Right, if we've all caught up then I may as well crack on with the story. Where was I again? Oh yeah ...

Forty-nine ... forty-eight ... forty-seven ...

I tried to ignore it, but the fog was everywhere I turned. Left, right and centre. Above and below. Up close and personal. Whether I liked it or not, I simply couldn't avoid it.

And I couldn't avoid tripping over my own feet either. Running at full pelt, my left hit my right before a combination of the two sent the rest of me tumbling. I hit the ground hard and rolled over. It hurt, but there was no time to feel sorry for myself. If I was going to escape then I had to keep moving. The minute (like most minutes tend to do) was disappearing fast. Which reminds me ...

Thirty-five ... thirty-four ... thirty-three ...

The howling started on thirty-two.

I had been warned about the wild wolves. How they stalked the compound and hunted their prey in packs. Now they were closing in. Getting ready to strike.

And I don't think I need to tell you who they were targeting!

Fear overwhelmed me and I kicked out in panic. My foot failed to connect with anything wolf-like, but I kicked out again. Better to be safe than sorry.

Twenty-two … twenty-one … twenty …

Scrambling up off the ground, I tried to put the wolves to the back of my mind as I pressed on wearily into the gloom. Where was the forest? Surely I should've reached it by now.

Ten … nine … eight …

I was slowing down. Sensing my weakness, the fog seemed to wrap itself around my body, squeezing the life out of me before I could resist. I carried on for a few more steps before I began to stagger. There was no end in sight, but I had reached the end regardless.

Five … four … three …

I was still two seconds shy of the full minute when my legs gave way from under me. To say I was tired was an understatement. I was beyond exhausted. Completely drained. An empty shell of a boy.

Escaping was never meant to be this hard.

The howling may have come to an end, but now a shrill, high-pitched screech-like feedback from a speaker was trying its best to fill the silence. Coming from somewhere above me, it wasn't long before that, too, stopped suddenly, only to be replaced by a voice.

'Well, that didn't go to plan now, did it?' giggled Odd.

No. Obviously not.

'Rules are there for a reason,' Odd continued. 'I am to be obeyed at all times. Do you understand that now, my child? Has it finally sunk in?'

I curled up into a ball, beaten and defeated. I had let

myself down. No, it was worse than that. Much, much worse. I had let the others down, too.

Dodge.

Mo.

Wheelie.

Angel.

They were my friends. I had promised them I would escape and yet I had failed at the first attempt. Maybe that was it. No more second chances. What if we were doomed to spend the rest of our lives with the strangest man we had ever had the misfortune to meet?

What if we were stuck on Odd Island forever?

'I am not a vindictive person, Twenty,' said Odd. 'Norman will come and get you. And then he will bring you home.'

I waited for what seemed like an eternity before the big lump finally arrived. He was wearing something over his face. A gas mask. That explained a lot. You didn't need a gas mask to pass through fog, but you did need it when faced with poisonous fumes powerful enough to knock you off your feet and strip you of all energy.

Barely breaking stride, Norman grabbed me by the ankle and set off back the way he had just come. It should've hurt as he dragged me along the ground, but I was too weak to notice.

'Bad luck,' Norman mumbled.

I think that's what he said anyway. Truth is, I couldn't be certain. Not that it mattered. Not compared to what had just happened.

My escape from Odd Island was over.

If I'm being honest though, it had never really begun.

29.'SAY HELLO TO OUR NEW ARRIVAL.'

At some point I must have passed out.

I knew this because I had just woken up. That's how these things work. You should ask a doctor if you don't believe me.

Opening one eye, I felt a sharp, stabbing pain in my forehead. It hurt so much that I closed it soon after and opened the other instead. Oh, that hurt too. I should've guessed. Makes sense when you think about it.

With both eyes tightly shut, I took a moment to recall everything that had happened. Odd had given me the chance to escape … and I had failed tragically. I didn't like to admit it, but that was the truth. I hadn't even made it to the forest. Maybe Odd had planned that all along. He knew about the fog and what it would do to me. How it sapped my energy and left me on my knees. And that was why I had ended up here.

Not that I knew where *here* actually was. And I wouldn't find out either. Not until I did the unthinkable and opened my eyes.

The first thing I saw was a bright light directly above me, shining straight at my face. I reached up and pushed it to one side. Ah, that was better. I could see now.

I was back where it had all begun. On a bed in the examination room. Like before, it was spotlessly clean and just as bare. I glanced over at the air vent, half expecting to see Dodge come crawling through at any moment. My heart sank when he didn't.

I wriggled my feet, relieved to find that they, like my wrists, were unrestrained. That was my cue to climb out of bed without a second thought. I knew it was a bad move when my legs immediately gave way and I collapsed in a crumpled heap. I took a breath and then tried again. With the aid of the bed frame, I managed to haul myself up and then stay there. My legs felt as weak as they had done out there in the fog, but that didn't stop me from shuffling slowly towards the door. It was only a few metres, but I had to lunge at the handle to stop myself from falling. To my surprise, it opened and I stumbled out into the corridor.

'Ah, good afternoon, Twenty.'

The door to Odd's bedroom was wide open and the man himself was stood in the doorway.

'Come. We have much to talk about,' he said, urging me to join him. 'No offence, but you look terrible, Twenty. Didn't you like it *outside*? Wasn't it all you expected?'

I followed Odd into his bedroom and collapsed onto the carpet. 'It wasn't the best day out I've ever had.'

'No, I don't suppose it was.' Odd began to grin as he sat down in his favourite chair. 'How was your sleep by the way?'

'I can't remember,' I shrugged. 'I wasn't awake for most of it.'

'That's the whole point,' chuckled Odd. 'You've been out for the count for almost twenty hours. You've missed three meals—'

'Lucky me,' I muttered under my breath.

'And a whole morning's chores,' continued Odd. 'You can make that up to me at some point. I hope that won't be a problem, will it?'

'I guess not,' I said wearily.

'Correct answer,' beamed Odd. 'Maybe you're not such a lost cause, after all. Maybe there is a light at the end of your particular troublesome tunnel. Nothing would bring me greater pleasure, Twenty, than to watch you develop into the fine young man I know you can be. A hard-working, upstanding member of our island community. A child I can be proud of.'

I nodded without thinking. Funnily enough, this seemed to please Odd immensely.

'I gave you the chance to leave, but you came back to us,' he said joyfully. 'That's a sign. A sign that you're meant to be here. And that's why I can't turn my back on you. Not now. Not ever.'

I screwed up my face. A sign. Odd was talking nonsense. Who was he trying to fool? Me? Or just himself?

'Norman will be here soon,' revealed Odd. 'He can take you back to your hut where you can rest for a while. Not too long, of course. Those chores won't complete themselves. Oh, here's my special boy now. And he's not alone.'

I looked over my shoulder … and almost jumped out of my skin. Norman was stood hunched over in the doorway. In front of him, however, dressed identically to all the other children in a blue boiler suit, was a girl.

No, not *just* a girl.

'Enter,' said Odd, ushering them both into his bedroom. 'Remember your manners, Twenty,' he added, glaring at me. 'Stand up and say hello to our new arrival.'

I stood up. That was the easy bit. The words, however, refused to come.

'Don't make me blast you with my child zapper!' said an irritated Odd. 'We've only just spoken about your disobedience. Say hello now or I'll be forced to punish you!'

'Hello,' I mumbled eventually.

'Hello yourself.' The girl pulled a face at me, confused. 'Fancy seeing you here—'

'That'll do,' said Odd, interrupting her mid-sentence. 'Manners are important, but I don't encourage small talk amongst my children. Nor big talk. None of the talks, in fact. You can run along now, Twenty, but remember what we spoke about. I've been kind to you, but kindness has a limit. This is your final warning. Your *final* final warning. As for you, Twenty-One, welcome to your new life. This is Odd Island. I'm sure you'll be very happy here …'

I was still stood rooted to the spot when Norman grabbed me by the collar and dragged me across the carpet. We left the bedroom and carried on along the corridor until we reached the exit to the Nerve Centre.

Norman opened the door. Fearful of being tossed out

into the courtyard, I took one last look at the new arrival.

The girl in Odd's bedroom wasn't Twenty-One.

No, she had a name.

And that name was Fatale De'Ath.

30.'NO TIME LIKE THE PRESENT.'

My head was spinning as I laid on my bed and tried to make sense of what had just happened.

Fatale De'Ath was here! On Odd Island! How could that be? The last time I had seen her was in the sewer. When was that? Three … four … five days ago? It was impossible to tell. Truth is, I had lost track of time the moment the handkerchief had been pressed to my face under Archie's Arch. Days weren't the same after that. They just merged into one long, continuous blur.

I, however, hadn't changed a bit.

I was still Hugo Dare. Agent Minus Thirty-Five. Codename Pink Weasel. I was a spy, not a prisoner. Everything on Odd Island was designed to erase the past from my mind, but I couldn't let it beat me. Not when everybody around me was struggling so badly. They may have been slowly fading away, but I had to stay sharp. Switched on. Ready for anything.

What I wasn't ready for, however, was Dodge. And that probably explains why I almost fell off my bed when the door to the hut swung open and in he wandered.

'Afternoon,' he said, smiling brightly. 'Daddy sent me to come and … are you okay, matey? You look like you've seen a ghost.'

I stood up and made my way over to the bucket. The last thing I wanted was for anybody else to listen in to our conversation. Especially if that *anybody else* was Ebenezer Odd.

'Not a ghost,' I replied. 'Just someone I know. A girl. A friend.'

'A girlfriend?' wondered Dodge.

'I didn't say that, did I?' I snapped back at him.

'Well, yes, you did,' shrugged Dodge. 'Kind of.'

'There's no kind of about it,' I muttered. 'She's a girl who I just happen to know. She's only just arrived. She's Twenty-One.'

Dodge's mouth fell open. 'Wow! What a coincidence!'

'I suppose,' I said, not convinced in the slightest. 'Unless she was sent here on purpose.'

'Children don't get sent here on purpose,' laughed Dodge.

'No, they don't, do they?' I had, of course. Not that I was about to tell Dodge that. Not yet, anyway. Maybe one day. When I had done what I had set out to do. When we had got off Odd Island.

If we ever got off Odd Island.

'Did you get to speak to her?' asked Dodge, derailing my train of thought.

'No, but I want to,' I replied. 'And as soon as possible.'

Dodge began to nod. 'Well, you know the old saying, matey.'

I screwed up my face. 'Let me think … erm … too many books spoil the bookcase? No? How about … never wipe your nose on a cow's tail? What? That's not even a saying? It is good advice, though—'

'There's no time like the present,' revealed Dodge.

Ah, *that* old saying. He was right, of course. If I wanted to speak to Fatale then I should just go and do it.

Dodge turned towards the door. 'What are you waiting for?'

I leapt up off the bucket and hurried over to him. I felt better now. Weak, yes, but at least I had a purpose. A reason to stop me from moping about and feeling sorry for myself.

And that reason was Fatale De'Ath.

I was about to leave the hut when Dodge placed a hand on my arm. 'I'm sorry, matey,' he whispered. 'About yesterday. I should have stood up to Odd and gone with you. We could've done it … you and me … together. Maybe we could've escaped.'

'Maybe,' I shrugged.

'I was just … you know … scared,' admitted Dodge. 'I'm scared all the time. I don't like it here, in the compound, but I don't like it out there either. I just want to go home. That's no excuse, though. I know I let you down.'

'Forget it,' I said. 'I know I have. Until you reminded me. But now I've forgotten it again. Listen, you're still my pal if that's what you're worried about.'

'Sweet.' Dodge was grinning from ear to ear as he pushed open the door. 'Remember, any time you need someone to crawl through the air vents, I'm your boy,' he added.

We bumped knuckles before we went our separate ways. Out in the courtyard, most of the children were busy at work.

Most … but not all.

Stood on the opposite side of the compound with two other girls that I didn't recognise, Fatale was watching me like a hawk as I made my way down the ramp.

'No time like the present,' I muttered to myself. With that, I set off across the courtyard. If I was lucky nobody would stop me.

And if I was unlucky …

I hadn't gone far when I came to a sudden halt. There was something blocking my way. Something small in size and yet massively irritating.

'Hello, friend,' said Priscilla.

I shifted from left to right, but she mirrored my moves. As small as she was, there was no way past.

'Hello, Two,' I sighed.

Priscilla appeared to visibly tremble. 'Don't call me that.'

'I thought that was your number,' I said, trying not to smile.

'It is … for now,' said Priscilla through gritted teeth. 'Although Daddy will soon reinstate me to One when I … I—'

'When you what?' I asked suspiciously.

'When I do everything I'm told,' said Priscilla quickly. I knew what she meant by that. If she continued to spy on me like Odd had demanded then she would soon be back in favour. 'What are you … um … doing now?' she mumbled awkwardly.

'What am I doing now?' I took a moment before I answered. Maybe it was time to have a bit of fun. 'I'm escaping,' I replied.

'Escaping?' Fatale cried.

'Not so loud,' I said, looking around. 'Yes, that's right. I'm escaping. Right now. This minute. You could even say that I've already escaped.'

Priscilla couldn't hide the grin that spread across her lips. 'Tell me more,' she whispered.

'Of course,' I said. 'I'll tell you everything. I mean, it's not as if you'll go and report back to Daddy, is it?'

Priscilla shook her head.

'You're one of us, aren't you?' I continued. 'We stick together. It's not our fault we've been kidnapped.'

'Not kidnapped,' frowned Priscilla.

'Yes kidnapped,' I insisted. 'What else would you call it?'

'Rescued,' Priscilla replied. 'Saved from ourselves. Daddy's a wonderful man who only brings joy and happiness to all those he encounters ...'

I groaned out loud. There was no helping some people, however hard I tried. And, however hard I tried, there was still no way past Priscilla.

'You promised to tell me more,' she said, poking me in the chest. 'How have you already escaped?'

I urged her to come closer before I spoke. 'Part of me might be stood here with you, but there's another part of me that escaped a long time ago,' I began. 'It's back home. Talking to my mum and dad. Hanging out in my shedroom.'

Fatale looked me up and down, confused. 'Which part of you is that?'

'My mind,' I said. 'And my body will follow it soon enough. When I figure out how.'

'I don't understand,' shrugged Priscilla.

'You wouldn't.' With that, I finally swerved around her and continued across the courtyard. Fatale still hadn't moved an inch. It wouldn't take me long to reach her now. Just a few more steps …

I was about to call out when someone else stepped in front of me. This time, however, the obstacle was taller, wider and far more menacing.

'Going somewhere?' sneered Buck.

The leader of the Savages was just as big and twice as ugly as the last time I had seen him.

'Yes, I was,' I replied honestly. 'Then something got in my way. Oh, that something was you. Feel free to shift at any time—'

'Stop talking!' Buck placed a hand on my shoulder and began to squeeze. 'Me and you … it's not over. I haven't finished with you yet.'

'Is that so?' I said, slipping out of his grasp. 'Because I finished with you a long time ago. The moment I tripped you up to be precise. You do remember that moment, don't you? Up until then you and the rest of your goons had been trying to choke me.'

'You deserved it,' smirked Buck. 'And what's going to happen to you next will be even worse. I've got a secret weapon.'

'Is it your breath?' I wondered. 'Because, powerful as that may be, it's not a secret. Everybody knows it stinks—'

Buck grabbed me by my boiler suit and dragged me towards him. 'I'm going to make you suffer.'

'No, you're not,' I argued. 'You're only tough when the rest of the Savages are right behind you. And, besides, you're not really sure what to make of me. I'm not like the other children. I'm unpredictable. Yes, I could always try and fight back, but I'm just as likely to do something like this …'

Raising myself up onto my tip-toes, I leant forward and kissed Buck on the forehead. It was both wet and sloppy with an extra dollop of dribble. The kind of kiss your least favourite aunt would usually reserve for special occasions. As I hoped, Buck's first reaction was to back away from me.

'Let me pass or I'll follow that up with a cuddle,' I remarked. 'I'm not joking. Is that a risk you're prepared to take?'

I smiled as Buck stepped to one side. That was easier than I expected. So easy, in fact, that he didn't even try and stop me as I continued across the courtyard.

Nearly there …

I was about to reach out and grab Fatale by the arm when a huge shadow passed over me. At first I thought it was Buck. Maybe he had changed his mind. Maybe he did want that cuddle after all.

Or maybe he didn't. Because it wasn't Buck at all.

It was Norman.

I tried to pretend I hadn't seen him, but that simply wasn't possible. Unlike the others, Norman didn't even have to *try* to block my path – he just did.

'Stop!' he said gruffly.

'I already have,' I replied. 'But, if it's okay with you, I think I'd like to start again.'

'Not okay,' Norman grunted. 'Work.'

'I am working,' I insisted. 'Anybody can see that. Oh, anybody except you. When are you getting those glasses I mentioned?'

Not for the first time, Norman lifted a hand to his face. 'Glasses.'

'That's right,' I nodded. 'You should ask Daddy to get you some. No, don't ask … *demand*. Go now. This minute. Don't worry about me. I can take care of myself.'

I moved swiftly before Norman could make sense of what I had said. First, I shimmied to my left before dodging to my right a split-second later. Not only did it leave Norman off balance, but it also gave me the opportunity to do the last thing either of us would ever have expected. Quick as a flash, I dropped to my knees and crawled between the big man's legs. I leapt up as soon as I emerged out the other side and started to walk.

Fatale had gone.

That was the last thing I saw before two huge hands gripped me firmly around the waist. Again I was on the move, but this time I was spun around in mid-air until I was facing in the opposite direction.

'Work,' ordered Norman, dropping me without warning. 'Now.'

Against my better judgment, I did as I was told. My chat with Fatale would have to wait. I mean, it wasn't as if we were going anywhere. Not yet, anyway. Seeing Fatale, however, had definitely reignited the spark in me to escape. Okay, so the other Survivors had skills that I could call upon, but she was different. She was sneaky and underhand and more than a little bit devious, all of which would no doubt come in useful when trying to get off the island.

I grabbed a brush and set about sweeping the compound. I would talk to Fatale later, I was sure of it. Somehow, I would find a way.

I *always* found a way.

I don't know if you've ever realised this, but sweeping up dust and debris for hours on end can be quite boring.

Oh, did I say *quite*? I meant to say *extremely*. Still, at least I had managed to stay out of trouble whilst doing it. That was a first. And about as good as it gets on Odd Island.

It was only when I got back to the hut, in fact, that anything even remotely interesting started to happen.

'What was that?' I asked, jumping up off the bed as a curious *tapping* sound echoed around us.

'Calm down, matey,' said Dodge. 'It was just a knock on the door. Nothing to get worked up about.'

'A knock on the door is exactly what you get worked up about,' argued Mo. 'Odd always walks straight in. Norman always walks straight in. Even Priscilla walks straight in. Nobody ever knocks.'

'Good point,' admitted Dodge. 'Maybe one of us should go and take a look.'

'Yes, maybe *you* should,' grinned Wheelie.

Dodge rolled his eyes before creeping slowly towards the door.

'B-B-Be careful,' warned Angel. 'It m-m-might be a trap.'

'Don't tell him that,' said Mo. 'He's scared enough already.'

'No, I'm not!' With that, Dodge pulled open the door and peeked outside. A moment later he knelt down and picked something up off the floor.

'What is it?' asked Mo.

'A note.' Dodge closed the door and passed me a slip of paper. 'It's for Hugo.'

Sure enough, *Twenty* was written in big letters on one side. Turning it over, I began to read.

'Who's it from?' wondered Wheelie.

I took a moment. 'Norman.'

'Norman?' Mo frowned at me. 'What does he want?'

'You're not going to believe this,' I said, shaking my head in amazement, 'but Norman's turned. He's one of us now. He wants to help me to escape.'

31. 'SHE'S JUST A GIRL.'

I laid the note on Wheelie's bed so that the other Survivors could all see it.

> *TWENTY,*
> *Meat me beetwen the huts in ten minites time.*
> *I can help you to excape.*
> *NORMAN.*

Everyone read it once and then read it again, largely because they couldn't quite believe what they were reading. Everyone except Angel. She was sat on the bucket so I picked up the note and took it over to her when the rest of them had finished. By the look on her face she wasn't convinced.

'That spelling is t-t-terrible,' she remarked.

'Is it?' I said, shifting awkwardly on the spot. 'I didn't realise.'

'Does anybody else find all this a little hard to believe?' asked Dodge.

'Yes, *everybody* else,' replied Mo. 'Norman didn't send that note and that's a fact.'

'Really?' I screwed up my face. 'Why not?'

'Why do you think?' Mo snapped back at me. 'Norman doesn't like you for a start.'

'Harsh ... but true,' grinned Wheelie.

'It's not just me,' I insisted. 'Norman doesn't like anybody. Or rather, he didn't. I've been talking to him a lot these past few days and got to know him quite well. You could almost say we're friends.'

'Dream on,' laughed Mo. 'Norman's only got one friend and that's Odd. There's no way he'll help you to escape. Especially after what happened yesterday when they let you go but you decided to come back.'

'Don't remind me,' I frowned. 'Okay, so maybe it's not Norman who wants to help me, but *somebody does*.'

'No, somebody wants to *meet* you,' said Mo, correcting me. 'There's a big difference. It might be a trap.'

'Well, there's only one way to find out ...' I switched my attention to Angel before Mo had a chance to disagree. 'Have ten minutes passed yet?' I asked.

'N-N-Not quite,' she replied. 'Why?'

'No reason,' I said sheepishly.

'You're going to meet them, aren't you?' said Dodge, grinning at me. 'Whoever sent this note.'

'Of course he is,' sighed Mo. 'It's the foolish thing to do, so why would he do anything else?'

I was about to object when Dodge wandered over and placed a hand on my shoulder.

'I wouldn't bother arguing if I was you, matey,' he said. 'Just go and do what you have to do. I'll even come with you if you like. Safety in numbers.'

I shook my head. 'Thanks, but no thanks. I think I'd rather go alone if that's alright with you. That way, if anything goes wrong it'll be me who has to take it on the chin.'

Dodge shrugged his shoulders. He looked deflated, but that didn't mean I was about to change my mind. Anything could happen outside, and if I got caught by Odd the punishment would be far worse than a simple blast of his child zapper. I had already been stuck in Isolation (albeit for twenty-three minutes) and had no wish to return there any time soon. More than that, though, I had no wish for Dodge to ever go there full stop.

'The t-t-ten minutes are up,' said Angel.

I nodded at her before heading for the exit. It wasn't quite seven o'clock yet so the door opened without Priscilla's pass. I peeked out first, wary of anybody who might be lying in wait. As far as I could tell, the courtyard was empty. The searchlight passed and I slipped outside, stopping only to close the door gently behind me. I stayed low until the searchlight passed again and then made my way around to the side of the hut. It was even darker there. So dark that I couldn't see the figure who was stood in the shadows.

'I was hoping you would show up.'

It wasn't Norman.

'You?' I sighed.

'Yes, me.' Buck walked forward until we were face-to-face. 'You look nervous,' he smirked.

'Not nervous,' I replied. 'Just disappointed. *Massively* disappointed. I was hoping to meet someone much, much larger but equally as stupid if I'm being honest. What are you doing here?'

'Waiting for you, of course,' revealed Buck.

That was the moment the penny dropped. 'Ah, don't tell me it was you who sent the note,' I groaned.

'It was me who sent the note,' grinned Buck, confirming my worst suspicions. 'I told you I hadn't finished with you … and now I'm going to rough you up good and proper!'

I began to shake my head. 'You and whose army?'

'*My* army!' announced a voice from somewhere behind Buck. 'Although, when all's said and done, I'm not really an army, am I?'

I tried not to smile as Fatale De'Ath emerged from out of the shadows.

'No, you're just a one woman wrecking machine,' I remarked. 'I am pleased to see you, though.'

'You won't be saying that in a minute,' said Buck, hopping up and down on the spot. 'Not when she duffs you up.'

'She won't duff me up,' I said calmly. 'Admittedly, she might do something weird like stick a finger up my nose or pull on my earlobes, but she won't really hurt me.'

'Yes, she will,' insisted Buck. 'She's like me. She's a Savage.'

'Is that true?' I couldn't hold back the frown as I turned to Fatale. 'You're a Savage? That's unfortunate.'

'Unfortunate for *you*,' snarled Buck. 'Unfortunate when she duffs you up.'

'You can say that as often as you like,' I sighed. 'It's still not going to happen.'

'Yeah, it is,' growled Buck.

'No, it's not,' I argued.

'Yeah, it is,' growled Buck for a second time.

I was about to speak again when Fatale beat me to it. 'No, it's really not,' she said firmly.

'What?' Buck's mouth fell open. 'But you said you would.'

'Did I?' mumbled Fatale. 'I mean, yes I did … kind of. I said I'd come out here with you because it sounded like fun. That was before I knew it was Stinky, though.'

Buck looked at me, confused. 'Stinky?'

'It doesn't matter,' I said hastily. 'All you need to know is that nobody's getting duffed up tonight.'

'Yes, they are,' spat Buck. 'Not one … but two. Both of you. That's what happens when you mess with a Savage.'

With that, Buck flew at Fatale and pushed her against the side of the hut.

'I really wouldn't do that,' I said, screwing up my face.

'Why not?' shrugged Buck. 'She's just a girl.'

Wow. Did he really just say that? Yes, he did. And now he was going to regret it.

'I'm just a girl?' repeated Fatale.

'You should probably think about apologising, Bucky Boy,' I suggested. 'And then crawl back to your hut as fast as your hands and knees will take you.'

'I'm … just … a … girl?' said Fatale again slowly. 'No, you must be mistaken. I'm not just *a* girl – I'm *the* girl!'

'Big deal,' remarked Buck. 'I'm not scared of you. And now I'm going to prove it.'

Oh dear. This was going to end badly. That was a fact. I'd give it three seconds … two … one …

Buck made the fatal error of making the first move. Without thinking, he held his breath and swung wildly, but it was easy to avoid. Ducking down, Fatale waited until his fist had cleared her head before she jumped up and grabbed him by his boiler suit. Before Buck could push her away she had flipped him onto his back and sat on top of him.

'Get off me!' he moaned.

'Not until you say sorry,' insisted Fatale.

Buck shook his head. 'Never.'

I knew Fatale wouldn't settle for that. 'What did you say I'd do, Stinky?' she asked me. 'Something like this …'

I watched in horror as Fatale stuck a finger up each of Buck's nostrils.

'Stop it,' he cried. 'I'm sorry … I'm sorry … I'm sorry …'

'I can't hear you,' laughed Fatale.

'Just let him go,' I said, glancing over my shoulder. They were making so much noise that it wouldn't be long before someone came to investigate. 'I still need to talk to you, Fatale.'

'And I still need to talk to you,' she said, agreeing with me. 'But first I'm going to show this dummy why he shouldn't be so rude about girls.'

Buck screamed out loud as Fatale pulled on his earlobes.

'We haven't got time for this,' I insisted. 'Let him go before it's too late …'

'Maybe it's too late already.'

I didn't need to turn around to know that there was someone stood behind me.

Typical.

I knew we'd get caught eventually … and I was right!

32. 'THAT IS AN ORDER.'

The someone stood behind me was Priscilla.

Also known as Two. Soon to be One again if she got her own way.

'Daddy doesn't like his children gathering outside in the dark,' Priscilla whined, wagging an accusing finger at us. 'And he certainly doesn't like you to be fighting.'

Fatale let go of Buck's ears and smiled her sweetest smile. 'We're not fighting,' she said innocently. 'I can't imagine anything worse. I'm just … um … playing.'

'And I'm not even doing that,' I added. 'I was just out on my early evening stroll and happened to be passing. So, if it's alright with you, Two, I think I'll call it a night and head on back to the—'

'Not so fast!' Marching forward, Priscilla continued to wag her finger until it flicked against the tip of my nose. 'You tell so many lies, Twenty, it's impossible to know when you're telling the truth.'

'Bit rude,' I frowned. 'And I thought we were friends—'

'Well you thought wrong!' hissed Priscilla. 'I wouldn't be friends with you if you were the last person on Odd Island.

Daddy made me do it, but I can't pretend a moment longer. It's unbearable. No, *you're* unbearable. And as for you, Twenty-One, I know fighting when I see it … and you were fighting! Why would you do that? You've only been here a day!'

'I don't know,' shrugged Fatale. 'It seemed like a good idea at the time. And then you came along and ruined everything.'

'Ruined everything? Oh, I've barely started,' said a smug Priscilla. 'I'm about to take the three of you to see Daddy. I wonder what he'll have to say about things.'

'You're going to take us to Odd?' I tried not to laugh as I reeled off the same line I had used just a few pages ago. 'You and whose army?'

'Me and *my* army.' Priscilla clicked her fingers and, right on cue, the ground began to shake as Norman appeared from behind one of the huts.

'Okay, you win,' I had to admit. 'That is a pretty good army. Shall we go now?'

I walked straight past both Priscilla and Norman as I set off across the courtyard. It felt strange to let the searchlight pass over me, but there was no need to avoid it anymore. Not now we had been caught.

I stopped at the entrance to the Nerve Centre and waited for the rest of them to catch up. Barging his way to the front, Norman flashed his pass and the door opened. I entered first, took several steps forward and then came to a sudden halt. One by one, the others all walked into the back of me. It was quite silly really, but I still found it amusing (even if no one else did).

'What's going on?' Stood in the doorway to his bedroom, Ebenezer Odd was cradling Mrs Snuggleflops in his arms like an unnaturally hairy baby. 'My, oh, my, this is unexpected,' he said, casting an eye over us as we made our way towards him.

'Not *that* unexpected,' replied Priscilla. 'I've brought you three naughty children, Daddy. Three naughty children for you to punish.' Priscilla paused. 'I've done well, haven't I?' she added, a little too desperately for my liking.

'I'll be the judge of that when you tell me what their crime is,' remarked Odd. He put Mrs Snuggleflops down on the carpet and closed the door behind us. I heard it *click* a moment later. We were trapped. 'I'm waiting …' said Odd, crossing his arms.

'I caught them fighting,' revealed Priscilla. 'Twenty-One was sat on top of Three. She was pulling on his ears—'

'And Twenty?' said Odd, pointing an accusing finger at me. 'Don't tell me he was involved.'

'Yeah, *don't* tell him I was involved,' I said, scowling at Priscilla.

Priscilla bit down on her lip, deep in thought. 'Well, he was there,' she said eventually. 'In the courtyard. He wasn't really doing much … but it was only a matter of time! That's what he's like, Daddy. A troublemaker. And that's why I brought him here.' Priscilla stuck her nose up in the air. 'And that's also why I deserve to be One,' she announced. 'I am your favourite, after all. I'll do anything you ask.'

'Is that what all this is about?' sighed Odd. 'Your number? How disappointing! So disappointing, in fact, that

I'm tempted to drop you down another. How would you feel about becoming Three?'

'Three?' Priscilla turned a deathly shade of white before our very eyes. 'No, not Three. Anything but Three. Three's the worst number imaginable!'

'Hey, that's my number you're talking about,' grumbled Buck. 'It's not that bad.'

'I can certainly think of worse,' I said, nodding at the Savage. 'Minus Thirty-Five for a start.'

'That's not even a proper number,' said Buck, confused.

'Maybe not in this life,' I said, winking at him. 'There's a lot about me you don't know though, Bucky Boy. Perhaps I'll tell you some time, when all this is over and you're not quite so angry—'

'Stop it! Stop it! Stop it!' barked Odd. 'We are not here to compare numbers. Norman, take Two back to her hut before I change my mind and turn her into a double digit.'

I kept one eye on Norman as he padded silently across the bedroom towards a horrified-looking Priscilla. 'You don't always have to do what Odd tells you,' I blurted out. 'You could say no from time to time. Go on. Just try it. It's only one word. Two letters …'

To my amazement, Norman stumbled to a halt. 'No,' he muttered under his breath.

'What is the meaning of this?' raged a furious Odd. 'You know the rules, Twenty. You don't call me Odd – you call me Daddy. And you don't tell Norman what to do either.'

'And neither should you,' I chipped in. 'Norman's a big boy now. No, a big man. A really big man. Like freakishly big. I'm sure he can think for himself.'

'No, he can't,' argued Odd. 'Norman prefers it when I do all his thinking. And I'll prove it. Take Two back to her hut, my special boy. Now.'

Norman hesitated for a moment before he started to move.

'You didn't even say please,' I said, shaking my head at Odd. 'Where did you leave your manners?'

'My manners?' A seething Odd glanced longingly at the child zapper in the corner of the room, before quickly changing his mind. 'Norman, forget about Two,' he said. 'Take Twenty to Isolation, instead. He can spend the night in there. That's the only way to punish a child like him.'

I watched as Norman changed direction and turned towards me. 'Odd doesn't care about you,' I said, scurrying backwards. 'Not in the slightest. He just treats you like his servant. He hasn't even got you any glasses.'

Norman took a moment to rub his eyes. 'Glasses?'

'My special boy doesn't need glasses,' remarked Odd. 'He's perfect in every way imaginable.'

'Except he can barely see,' I argued. 'You would know that if you bothered to ask him. But, no, you'd rather spend your days shuffling about Odd Island, pretending to be important.'

'Right, that's two days in Isolation,' cried Odd. 'See him out, my special boy.'

'Don't do it, Norman,' I said firmly.

Unsure what to do next, Norman chose the easy option and simply stared at the ceiling.

'Three days,' shouted Odd, stamping his slipper. 'Take him now, my special boy.'

'Don't do it,' I said again.

'Four days!' yelled Odd.

'Don't do it,' I said for a third time.

'A week!' squealed Odd. 'A month! A year! Forever! Remove him this instant, my special boy. That is an order.'

'You don't take orders, Norman,' I said. 'You can think for yourself ... do what you like ... go where you want ... say more than one word occasionally ... whoa!'

Without warning, Norman dropped his head and charged at me like a raging bull in tight clothing. It took me by surprise, so much so that my only option was to dive to one side at the last moment. Norman missed me completely, but hit something nevertheless. Moving at speed, he tripped over Mrs Snuggleflops, who was curled up on the carpet, and then collided with his only friend on the island.

Ebenezer Odd.

Rolling over, I could barely believe my eyes as Odd flew backwards and slammed into the wall behind him. Ouch! That looked painful. And it would've been me who was hurting now if I hadn't shifted out the way a split-second earlier.

'What have you done?' shrieked Priscilla. She scowled at me as she hurried across the room to tend to the crumpled figure of Odd. 'I'll never forgive you if there's anything wrong with him.'

'There was a lot wrong with him to begin with,' I muttered. 'Getting walloped by his not-so-special boy can't have made much difference.'

Norman clenched his fists as if he was about to come at me again. He was distracted, though, by the sound of a panic-stricken Priscilla.

'You wicked, wicked boy!' Not only was that aimed at yours truly, but she was also glaring at me with such intensity that I feared her eyes might burn a hole in my forehead. 'You've done it now,' she continued, wiping the tears away. 'You've really gone and done it.'

I screwed up my face. 'I've done lots of things. You might have to narrow it down a bit.'

'This is your fault!' cried Priscilla, jabbing a finger at me in despair. 'Daddy is … dead! And it was you who killed him!'

33.'THIS IS THE WORST DAY OF MY LIFE!'

Norman dropped to his knees and started to cry.

And when I say cry, I mean cry. Not just the odd sniffle and little whimper. No, this was much, much more than that. Norman had big tears running down his face, snot trickling out of both nostrils and huge droplets of dribble dripping from his chin. Okay, so I knew he liked Odd – I just didn't know he liked him that much.

'Are you sure he's really dead?' I asked, wandering over for a closer look. 'He might just be a little sleepy.'

'Get away from him!' screeched Priscilla. 'You're not a doctor!'

'You don't know that,' I argued. 'I could've been anything before Odd Island. A doctor? An astronaut? Maybe even a spy?'

This seemed to confuse Priscilla enough for her to let me pass. Kneeling down on the rug, I pressed a hand to Odd's chest and immediately felt it rise. So I was right. He wasn't dead at all; he was just out cold. Which, all things considered, was probably a good thing (I repeat, probably).

I was about to stand up and reveal the (highly debatable) good news when Fatale knelt down beside me. 'What are you doing, Stinky?' she whispered in my ear.

'Just checking that he's okay,' I replied. 'And he is. Yes, he's currently out for the count, but he'll wake up eventually—'

'Shush.' Fatale put a hand over my mouth. 'That may be the truth,' she began, leaning in closer, 'but not everybody needs to know that. Do you catch my drift, Stinky?'

'Unfortunately so,' I mumbled. I removed her hand before I spoke again. 'This sounds like one of your highly dubious plans. The kind that gets us both into a whole heap of trouble.'

'Correct,' nodded Fatale. 'That's exactly what it is. If Norman and Priscilla both think that Odd is dead then they'll be too busy mourning him to notice what we're up to.'

'And what will we be up to?' I asked, fearing the worst.

'Getting off this rotten island, of course,' grinned Fatale. 'And don't tell me it's not as easy as that—'

'It's not as easy as that,' I moaned.

'No, it *wasn't* as easy as that,' Fatale insisted. 'It is now. Especially now that I'm here. We're the dream team, Stinky. We can do anything if we put our minds to it. Which is why I think it's best for you to say that darling Daddy is well and truly—'

'Dead!' I blurted out. I stood up at the same time and walked away from Odd's body. 'Sorry to be so blunt, but Daddy is no longer with us. He's passed over to the other side. He has sadly departed. Still, I'm sure we'll all get over it. I know I have.'

'How can you say that?' sobbed Priscilla. 'This is the worst day of my life!'

I patted her awkwardly on the head. Fatale was right – Norman and Priscilla were distracted. Certainly too distracted to worry about what the rest of us were doing.

'Time to leave,' said Fatale, winking at me as she crept over to the door. She pulled on the handle, but it refused to open. 'Do we need a pass?' she asked.

I nodded. 'Yes … and I've got one. I've just not got it with me. It's hidden under the bucket in the hut. And we're not. In the hut, I mean. Or under the bucket. So, the fact that I've got a pass isn't really that useful.'

'Good story, Stinky,' sighed Fatale, rolling her eyes at me. 'Really interesting. So, what now? How do we get out of here?'

'There is one way.' I moved over to the air vent in the wall. To my surprise I could hear noises coming from behind it. Strange scraping sounds. Identical to those I had first heard in the examination room. 'Surely not,' I said, pressing my ear up to the metal grille that covered the vent. 'I mean, that would be absolutely … whoa!'

I backed away as the grille began to shake and shudder before it eventually fell to the carpet. A moment later a head appeared in its place.

'Hello, matey,' said Dodge, gasping for breath. 'I thought I might find you in here. What's going down?'

I stepped to one side so he had a good view of the

bedroom. 'Odd's going down, that's what,' I replied.

'Wowsers!' Dodge didn't waste a second in crawling out of the vent. 'Is he … you know …?'

'Yes, I do know and he's not, 'I said quietly. 'But Norman and Priscilla think otherwise. That's why they're both so upset. It's also why they haven't realised that you've come to rescue us.'

'Rescue you?' Dodge pulled a face. 'I never said I was here to rescue you.'

'You just did,' I remarked. 'I heard it with my own ears. Besides, it's not as difficult as it sounds. We can get out the same way you just got in. You can lead us to safety through the air vent.'

'Are you being serious?' Dodge didn't even wait for me to reply as he clambered back into the tiny opening. 'Of course you are. Why did I even bother asking? Fine. I'll do it. Don't blame me if you get stuck, though. You're not as thin as me.'

'Rude,' muttered Fatale. Raising herself onto her tiptoes, she followed Dodge into the vent face-first. 'Okay, not that rude,' she had to admit. 'Give me a shove, Stinky. Don't hold back. As hard as you can.'

I grabbed her by the ankles and began to push. I was still pushing, in fact, when somebody spoke in my ear. 'What about me?'

I glanced over my shoulder and saw Buck stood behind me. He had been quiet all the time we had been in Odd's bedroom, which was just the way I liked him. Now, however, he had found his voice.

'I want to escape as well,' he insisted. 'But there's no way I can fit through there. I'm too big. Even my head would get stuck.'

'You could always chop it off,' I suggested. 'No, scratch that. Far too messy.'

'Come on, Stinky,' said Fatale, urging me to join her. 'It's not that tight in here when you get used to it.'

I was about to make my move when Buck grabbed me by the arm. 'You're not going anywhere,' he said angrily. 'If I can't get out of here then neither can you.'

I took a breath. I thought he might try something like this. I didn't blame him, though. Not really. But that didn't mean I was about to let him stop me.

'Don't do that,' I said calmly.

'Why not?' growled Buck.

'Well, it hurts for a start,' I replied. 'Also, if you let me go and I *do* manage to escape then I'll make sure I come back and get you. *All* of you.'

Buck's grip began to weaken. 'I don't think I can trust you.'

'And I don't think you really have a choice,' I shrugged. 'All you have is my word, but let me tell you something, Bucky Boy. I'm not like the rest of these children and I didn't end up on Odd Island by accident. Yes, I was kidnapped, but that was all my own doing. I needed to get here. And now I have, I want to go. And you have to let me. It's the best thing for both of us. Do you trust me now?'

Buck hesitated for a moment before releasing his grip. 'Promise that you'll come back and get me,' he said sadly.

'I promise,' I said, scrambling into the opening. 'Now, I don't want to rub it in but I could really do with a shove right now. You can take some of that anger out on my shoes if you like …'

I had barely finished my sentence before Buck did just that. Pushing hard against my heels, I flew along the air vent until I eventually came to a halt when I crashed into Fatale.

'Oh, nice of you to join us, Stinky,' she said. 'It's really hot in here.'

'It'll be even hotter if Odd wakes up,' I warned her. 'Let's keep moving.'

I took my own advice and began to slowly work my way along the vent. It was dark in there, but at least I had Fatale to guide me. And Fatale had Dodge. What could possibly go wrong?

We took a number of turns. Left and right and then left again. I crossed my fingers that Dodge knew where he was going. Then I uncrossed them a moment later because it only made crawling even more difficult than it already was.

'How much further?' panted Fatale.

'Not far,' Dodge insisted. 'It's just around this bend.'

'You said that two bends ago,' Fatale grumbled. 'You must think I'm stupid.'

'No comment,' muttered Dodge under his breath.

I tried not to laugh. Laughing would only use up air and I was starting to wonder how much of that we actually had left. Not only that, but my knees and elbows were burning so much as they rubbed against the walls of the vent that I feared they could even set alight. This had to stop. We couldn't keep on crawling forever. Before long we would have to …

I saw a light in the distance and my heart leapt. Next thing I knew Dodge had completely disappeared from view. Fatale followed soon after.

Two down. Me to go.

I kept on crawling until I left the vent behind and found myself stranded in mid-air. Gravity kicked in immediately and I began to fall. It was a hard landing, but I was so pleased to be out in the open that I barely noticed.

'You know when people say that was easier than they expected,' began Fatale, stretching her legs beside me. 'Well, those same people have clearly never crawled through an air vent before.'

I sat up and looked around. We were on the other side of the Nerve Centre, just out of range of the searchlight. If I strained my neck I could see the huts. Unsurprisingly, they were just where I had left them.

'Stop dreaming, Stinky,' said Fatale, pulling me to my feet. 'We've got a job to do.'

Dodge took the lead. Like his name suggested, he moved swiftly in and out of the shadows as he made his way towards our hut. Fatale went next and I brought up the rear. I had done it so many times by now it was a breeze.

'It's locked,' frowned Dodge, as I joined both him and Fatale at the top of the ramp.

Of course it was. It was gone seven in the evening. But that didn't mean that there was no way in.

I knocked three times. If the others had any sense they

would use the pass we had stolen from Priscilla. I knocked again when I realised they might not be that smart. And then kept on knocking until Mo finally opened the door.

'Oh, it's you,' she remarked. 'You're back.'

'Not for long,' I said, diving inside. Dodge and Fatale had already walked in behind me by the time I had picked myself up off the floor. 'We're leaving,' I announced. 'All of us. We've got a pass ... and that means we can get off Odd Island.'

'What are you talking about?' said Wheelie. 'Slow down and—'

'No, don't slow down – speed up!' I said, butting in. 'We have to move now and we have to move fast.'

Mo and Angel both did as I suggested and hurried towards the door. Wheelie, however, stayed exactly where he was.

'What are you waiting for?' I cried out. 'Dodge, grab his wheelchair. I'll help him—'

'There's no point,' said Wheelie, shaking his head. 'I'm not going with you ... and there's nothing you can do to change my mind!'

34. 'THERE'S NO TURNING BACK NOW.'

Ebenezer Odd would wake up eventually.

Sooner rather than later most probably. That was a fact. And that was also why we couldn't afford to waste another second. Or another one after that. Or …

Get on with it, Hugo!

'We haven't got time for this,' I blurted out. 'Why are you being so difficult?'

'I'm not,' shrugged Wheelie. 'And I'm not stopping any of you from leaving.'

'Yes, you are,' I argued. 'You're stopping us by refusing to come along.'

'I don't think that's how it works,' Wheelie replied.

'Listen,' began Mo, pushing me to one side so she could get closer to Wheelie's bed. 'I don't like agreeing with Hugo – it goes against everything I stand for – but he's right. We're not going anywhere without you. You're one of us. We're Survivors. You, me, Hugo, Dodge and Angel … oh, and whoever that is,' said Mo, gesturing towards the door.

'Me?' Fatale blew out in frustration as she looked back into the hut. 'I'm just someone who'd rather get out of here than stand around chatting.'

'Also known as Fatale,' I added. 'She's with me. She's a—'

'Friend,' finished Fatale. 'And friends stick together. So, if you lot are all friends, and you're all in agreement, I say we smash your awkward pal over the head with the bucket and then carry him out the door before he—'

'Whoa! That's not going to happen,' I said, interrupting Fatale mid-flow. 'But we *are* going to do something.'

All eyes turned towards me as I sat down on the edge of Wheelie's bed. The cogs had barely started turning, however, before Fatale interrupted the magic.

'Stinky,' she said abruptly. 'We haven't got all day.'

'I know,' I snapped back at her. 'I'm coming. We're *all* coming.'

'We're not,' insisted Wheelie, shaking his head. 'Whatever any of you say or think, we all know there's an elephant in the room—'

'That's just Mo,' I said. 'Just don't call her that to her face.' I was trying to lighten the mood, even if my own mood took a sudden dip when Mo punched me on the arm.

'I'm talking about my wheelchair,' frowned Wheelie. 'I can't escape in that. I'll never make it. Not out there … beyond the fence … on four wheels.'

'That's nonsense,' I argued. 'Everybody knows that four wheels are better than two … erm … legs.'

'In a car, perhaps,' agreed Wheelie. 'But not a wheelchair. What happens when we reach the forest? I'll just grind to a halt. And grinding to a halt means we'll all get caught.' Wheelie leant forward and gripped my arm. 'If just one of us can escape then that might be enough. One can get help. One can go to the police. One can tell everyone about Odd Island. It doesn't matter who it is. But it won't be me.'

'Or m-m-me,' added Angel.

'What?' I screwed up my face as I turned towards the quietest of the Survivors. And then screwed it up some more because at least it stopped me from screaming out loud. 'Not you as well,' I moaned. 'This can't be happening. Will somebody please pinch me so I can wake up ... ouch!'

I might have said it ... but that didn't mean I was expecting anybody to actually do it!

'Sorry about that, matey,' mumbled Dodge awkwardly, 'but this is real.'

'I'll stay w-w-with Wheelie,' insisted Angel. She took hold of my hand and smiled. 'Good l-l-luck, Hugo,' she said softly. 'Good l-l-luck all of you.'

I tried to smile back at her, but it wasn't easy. If anything, it looked as if I was trying to stop myself from burping.

'We really need to get out of here, Stinky,' said Fatale, hopping up and down on the spot.

Glancing over my shoulder, I gave her a thumbs-up. 'I'm not happy about this ... but ... let's go! As for you two,' I said turning back to Angel and Wheelie. 'I won't leave you here forever. That's a promise.'

With that, I hurried out of the hut. That was the second promise I had made that day. They were starting to add up. As was the pressure on me to escape.

'What's wrong?' asked Fatale, as I crouched down beside her on the ramp. 'You're not crying, are you?'

'Of course not.' I stopped and wiped a hand across my face. 'I've just got something caught in my eye. Something big. Like a … um … bird.'

'A bird?' Fatale snorted. 'You've got a bird in your eye? And I thought *I* was the weird one—'

'Shush you two.' Pushing her way to the front, Mo pointed up at the guards in the watchtower. 'They'll hear us if you're not careful.'

'I'm not so sure,' I said, staring at them with intent. 'Nothing would surprise me about Odd Island anymore. Why would the guards be any different? They're probably not even real.'

The scowl on Mo's face seemed to suggest she didn't agree. 'Would you like to go and find out?' she asked sternly.

'Not today, thank you,' I replied hastily. 'No, our best course of action is to hide here in the shadows until the searchlights pass and then we can make a run for it. Wait … any second … go, go, go!'

This time I took the lead. Keeping low to the ground, I stayed out of sight as I moved swiftly towards the watchtower. It wasn't long before I came out the other side. From there, it was a short sprint to the fence.

'Don't touch it,' warned Mo, once the other three had caught me up. 'You'll get electrocuted.'

'Will I?' Kneeling down beside the fence, I took a moment to study it a little closer. 'We only think it's electrically charged because Odd told us,' I said. 'We now know, however, that Odd lies about everything.'

'Not everything, matey,' remarked Dodge, grimacing at me. 'Just most things.'

It was a good point … and yet I still chose to ignore it.

I took a quick breath and then reached out with both hands, wrapping my fingers around the groove in the fence. To my relief, nothing happened. No shock. No frazzle or fry. No fear.

I wiped the sweat from my forehead before turning to Mo. 'Told you so.'

'Lucky guess,' she frowned. She was right, of course, so I quickly changed the subject.

'We need to find the secret door where Norman let me out,' I said. Standing up, I began to work my way along the fence. 'It can't be that hard to find …'

'No, you're right, matey,' replied Dodge. 'And that's because I've found it.'

I shuffled over to him and saw a small control panel above a tiny handle. Both were easy to miss if you weren't looking in the right place.

'Who's got the pass?' I said, holding out my hand.

'Not me,' shrugged Dodge.

'Or me,' said Mo.

'Or me,' said Fatale to my dismay. Thankfully, she didn't leave it long before she changed her mind. 'Oh, did you say pass? Yes, I've got that. I grabbed it from under the bucket when you lot were getting all sentimental. Don't look at me like that, Stinky. You can have it now …'

Fatale threw it at me – rather than *to* me – and I snatched it out of the air.

'This is it.' I took a breath before pressing the pass up to the panel. Then I took another because that's how breathing works. In … out … in … out. Nice and simple. 'There's no turning back now,' I said, trying to keep my cool.

The door began to open.

'Cut it out, Hugo,' grumbled Mo. 'This isn't some kind of rubbish action movie. Nobody's sat on the edge of their seat. There's no dramatic music.'

'I can whistle if you like,' laughed Fatale, stepping through the door. 'Right, what are you all waiting for? See you at the finishing line, losers.'

She started to run before I had a chance to warn her about the fog. Fearful of being left behind, I took off after her as fast as I could. My lungs were burning, but it felt good to stretch my legs and pump my fists. I drew level with Fatale, surprised to see that she was still laughing. It made me laugh, too.

'We're doing it!' cried Dodge, as he appeared from nowhere and overtook us. 'We're actually escaping from Odd Island!'

Even Mo was smiling now. I smiled back at her and she switched it to a frown.

'Team work makes the dream work,' grinned Fatale. She was right; we did make a good team. If only her father wasn't Deadly De'Ath.

And then, as if by magic, we all began to slow. We had reached the fog. It wasn't so easy to spot in the dark, but there it was. As thick as ever and practically impenetrable.

'This isn't just fog,' I warned the others. 'Norman was

wearing a mask when he came to take me back to the compound. And there's only one reason you'd wear a mask ...'

My sentence trailed off as everybody came to the same conclusion as I had.

'It's some kind of poisonous gas,' Mo blurted out. 'Pull your boiler suits up and cover your nose and mouth. And whatever you do, try not to breathe ...'

I did as she asked before pressing on into the unknown. The gas, however, had already started to affect me. Without warning, my vision blurred and a strange aching sensation appeared in my legs. I glanced over at the others. Dodge looked like he was struggling to carry his own bodyweight, whilst Mo couldn't stop rubbing her eyes. Only Fatale appeared unfazed. Striding forwards, she took the lead as the rest of us slipped slightly behind.

'Did you hear that?' asked Dodge, his voice distorted by the collar of his boiler suit.

I nodded. It was a cry of anguish. Horrible to listen to yet impossible to ignore.

'Wild wolves?' whispered Mo.

I shook my head. Yes, they howled, but surely not like that. This noise had come from something far, far bigger than any wolf.

As one, we stopped and turned around. Something was coming up behind us. If it was any smaller we would never have seen it through the gas, but this was huge.

'Is that what I think it is?' I muttered, fearing the worst.

'Not what ... *who*,' replied Fatale.

'Norman,' remarked Dodge. 'He's looking for us.'

'He *was* looking for us,' said Mo, correcting him. 'Something tells me, however, that he doesn't need to look anymore ...'

35.'DON'T COME BACK.'

Norman was edging closer with every massive stride.

Like yesterday, he was wearing a mask. Unlike yesterday, though, his fists were clenched and his arms were above his head as he stormed through the gas. He was raging. Anybody could see that. Even the four of us, and we could barely see at all.

'What now, matey?' asked Dodge, shifting nervously on the spot. 'Fight or flight?'

I didn't know how to answer that. We would struggle to wrestle Norman to the ground, but then we couldn't outrun him either. We were weak and getting weaker by the second. And, quite simply, he wasn't. He was Norman. There was no stopping him.

'What now, matey?' repeated Dodge, more on edge than ever.

'Now we split,' replied Mo, filling the silence. 'You two go one way,' she said, pointing at me and Fatale, 'and we'll go the other. Norman can only follow one pair ...'

'Leaving the other pair free to get away.' I didn't like the sound of it, but it made sense. It also left me with a difficult decision to make. At a guess, Norman would reach us in about eleven seconds time … ten … nine … eight-and-a-half … 'Let's do it,' I said hastily. 'With any luck, we'll meet up on the other side of the forest. If not—'

'Take care, matey,' said Dodge, stopping me mid-sentence. At the same time, he and Mo changed direction and swerved to their right. I watched them for a moment before turning back to Fatale. She was already on the move so I took off after her. I struggled to pick up speed, but I blamed that on the metal chains that had been attached to my ankles and the quicksand that I was wading through. That was what it felt like at least. Even if it wasn't true.

I couldn't let the gas beat me. With that in mind, I concentrated on the voice inside my head. You know the one. It tells you what to do and how to do it. Right now, the message was short and sweet.

Keep going.

Nobody needed to remind me that this was our best chance to escape. If we didn't, and Norman took us all back to the compound, then Odd's first response would be to increase security. Maybe the gate really would be electric after that. Maybe the guards would finally wake up and do something for a change. Norman was sure to find Priscilla's pass. That was inevitable. As were the various ways to punish me that would follow. Repeated blasts of the child zapper … another force-feeding by the Savages … Isolation. They were all options. Or maybe the food would just get worse. No, that wasn't possible. Still, whatever the outcome, the chance to escape may never arise again. Not like this. We were so close.

I peered over my shoulder and caught sight of Norman before he changed direction and disappeared from view. He had made his choice and followed Mo and Dodge. I didn't know whether to laugh or cry. Yes, the plan had worked, but there was no way I wanted my two friends to get captured instead. If anything the thought of it spurred me on even more. I had been given a free run to get off the island and that was what I'd do. I had made too many promises to fail now.

I was still caught up in my own thoughts when I crashed into Fatale. Either I had sped up without knowing or she had slowed down.

Unfortunately for the pair of us, I hadn't sped up.

I knew there was something wrong when Fatale went tumbling to the ground.

'Are you okay?' I asked, crouching down beside her.

I was hoping for a quick-fire reply, a snappy answer, even a stupid comment. What I got, however, was a single word. Quiet and distant.

'No.'

I watched in horror as Fatale curled up into a ball.

'Whoa! Don't do that!' I cried. 'This isn't nap time. We've got to keep going.'

Maybe Fatale couldn't hear me. Or she was just ignoring me. Either way, she didn't respond.

'I'll carry you,' I said, trying to pick her up. 'Put your hands around my neck. You can't be that heavy.'

Turns out, she was. Or at least, she *felt* like she was. Just like me, the gas had taken its toll on her. It was attacking her senses and beating her down. And there was nothing she could do to fight back.

'Go,' Fatale whispered.

'Not without you.' I heard a noise and turned sharply. Was it Norman? Or was it the wild wolves? Whichever, I had to keep moving. 'I can't leave you here,' I insisted.

'You have to.' With that, Fatale closed her eyes. 'Remember, if just one of us gets out, we can all get out. You can be that one, Stinky. No pressure,' she added with a giggle.

I knew then that Fatale's fight was well and truly over. There was nothing I could do to help her.

I, however, wasn't Fatale.

Clambering to my feet, I put my head down and set off again. Somehow, I still had more to give. Don't get me wrong; I was hardly jumping for joy with a spring in my step. For the sake of the others, though, if nothing else, I had to keep going.

I took short, sharp breaths into my boiler suit as I pressed on through the gas. Every time I thought I was about to reach the forest, the forest seemed to move further away from me. How was that even possible? I wasn't going backwards; I was moving forwards. Always forwards.

Or so I thought.

Suddenly I felt completely lost. I started to spin around, desperate to get my bearings. Had I somehow changed direction without realising? Veered off course by accident? My head said no, but I wasn't convinced that my head could be trusted. Not anymore.

I only stopped spinning when I slammed into something hard and slumped to the ground. What was it? A tree? No, it was wider than that. More like a wall. Reaching out, I let my fingers brush against its surface. It felt hard to touch, not brick or wood, but metal. I pressed my shoulder against it, but it held firm. No way past.

I stayed on my knees and chose left over right. Then I began to crawl. I kept going until I stumbled across something so unexpected that it completely blew my mind.

It was a door.

Now I was really confused. Why was there a door in a wall in the middle of all this poisonous gas?

Like most doors I had come across in my young life, this one had a handle. Gripping it tightly, I gave it the firmest yank I could muster. I didn't expect it to open. No, that would've been far too easy.

And guess what? It didn't.

The door was locked. My heart sank ... and then leapt almost immediately when I spotted a key in the hole. I turned it and waited for the *click*. Again, it was far too easy. Still, here goes nothing ...

I was about to pull on the handle when a jolt of pain surged up and down my leg. There was something heavy resting on my ankle. Something heavy like a bare foot.

There was only one person on Odd Island who was daft enough to be out and about with no shoes on.

The pressure eased and I rolled on to my back. Gas or no gas, there was still no mistaking the monstrous man mountain that was Daddy's special boy. For a moment,

Norman just stood there, towering over me. Then he spoke. At least, I think he did.

'Dome ... comb ... pack,' I said, trying to decipher his words. 'If that's what you're saying then I haven't got a clue what it means.'

Norman glared at me as he slowly removed his mask.

'Don't come back,' he grunted. With that, he turned around and walked away. I watched as he disappeared into the gas. I guessed he was heading back to the compound. Back to Ebenezer Odd. Back to where he belonged.

Unlike me.

Grabbing blindly for the door handle, I pulled down as hard as I could. I was still clutching hold of it when the door swung to one side and I fell through the opening. The first thing that hit me was an icy blast of cold air. It was enough to take my breath away, not that I had much to begin with.

Using what little strength I had left, I scrambled wearily to my feet and took my first stumbling step. I tried to rub my eyes, but they had glazed over and I could barely see. Not to worry. My other senses told me that everything felt different the moment I had passed through the door. The gas, for one thing, seemed to have vanished. Which would have been the best news ever if I hadn't lifted my foot without thinking.

That was when I took a tumble.

It was only my second step, but that was still one step too many as the ground disappeared from beneath my feet. Ok, so it wasn't the longest of drops, but it was still enough to scare me silly before I finally touched down. At least the landing was soft. Grass, both damp and overgrown. That alone was enough to get me thinking. This was the first grass I had come across on Odd Island, but that hopefully meant I was getting closer to the water. Then what? Was there a boat tied up there? A canoe or a rubber dinghy? Even an old wooden raft would've been better than nothing.

There was a fierce throbbing pain in the side of my head when I lifted my face out of the grass and forced my eyes to open. It was dark, just like it had been on the other side of the door, but this was a different kind of dark. Now I could see stars in the sky. Clouds and ... what was that? No, it couldn't be. Not a ... bird?

With the pain increasing with every passing second, I let my eyes close as I struggled wearily to my feet. Staggering from side to side, heading unknowingly into the unknown, I had no other option but to keep moving. I barely noticed as the grass beneath my feet turned to concrete. I was struggling now, stumbling and staggering with every step. Even with my eyes closed, a bright light was enough to stop me in my tracks. I put my hands in front of my face to block it out. This was no searchlight, though. This was lower down. At eye level. It was getting bigger and brighter and ...

It was coming straight at me.

The shrill blast of a horn jerked my senses into life. The light was about to hit me when I shuffled slightly to one side. Something fast *whooshed* past me at speed before I tripped over my own feet. I fell again, but this time there was no getting up.

I could hear more horns, but each one seemed to grow

fainter by the second. Before I knew it, blood was rushing around my ears, blocking out all other sounds. I was drifting … in … and out … in … and out …

'Cynthia, come quickly.' That was a man's voice. Not Odd. Not Norman. Somebody else. Somebody … normal. 'You have to see this,' the man continued. 'There's a boy in our garden.'

I guessed he was talking about me.

'A boy?' That was a woman, her voice distant. 'In our garden? What's he doing?'

'Not much,' replied the man honestly. 'I think he may be unconscious.'

I wasn't. Close perhaps, but not quite.

'I'll call the police,' called out the woman. 'You can never be too careful these days.'

'No, wait.' The man seemed to hesitate before he spoke again. 'I've got a better idea. Call the Big Cheese. He'll know what to do.'

The Big Cheese.

Also known as the Chief of SICK. My boss.

I wanted to scream *yes*, but even whispering it was beyond me. Instead, I took a breath and gave in to the inevitable. All of a sudden, it felt as if a switch had been flicked and my whole body had stopped working.

It was over. But I had done it. Escaped from Odd Island. Hadn't I?

36.'ARE YOU STILL IN THE ROOM?'

I was laid flat on my back when I finally woke up.

I blinked twice and feared I was back where it had first begun. Strapped to the bed in the examination room on Odd Island. Panic swept over me before I looked again and quickly changed my mind. That room had been painted white from floor to ceiling and spotless in every way imaginable. This one, however, wasn't. The walls were either orange or yellow in colour and covered in a wide array of framed pictures. Galloping horses mainly. As well as the occasional water buffalo. There was also a small wooden table beside me with a bulging fruit bowl, a cracked vase of wilting flowers and two plastic chairs to keep it company.

Oh, and there were windows.

I hadn't seen a window in days. It was only now that I realised how much I missed them. Okay, maybe not that much judging by the damp and dismal weather that lurked outside.

I moved my arms and shuffled my feet. I wasn't strapped in. And if I wasn't strapped in then there was nothing stopping me from standing up and wandering across the room.

My head was spinning as I swung my legs over the side of the bed and planted both feet firmly on the ground. I was dressed in a long white robe. (Think hospital gown. That's not an order, though. You don't have to do it if you don't want to.)

One breath later and I was ready to take my first steps.

I stopped before I had even started.

I could hear voices. They were coming from somewhere behind the door, increasing in volume with every passing second. Whoever it was, they were about to enter the room.

Not if I had anything to do with it …

My first thought was to use the bed to block the entrance. That was easier said than done, though. The bed shifted a little, but at the speed I was going it would probably take me at least twenty-three minutes to get it all the way to the door. That was far too long. Fact. For all I knew I might not even have twenty-three seconds.

I skipped from Plan A to Plan C without breaking stride for B. Now I needed a weapon. I looked around and narrowed it down to three things. One of the chairs. The vase. And the fruit bowl.

No contest.

The chair was too awkward and the vase was too small. The fruit bowl, however, was exactly what I wanted. Not only was it a perfectly formed weapon in its own right, but it also contained at least ten other weapons inside (also known as the fruit).

Without missing a beat, I snatched the bowl off the table and hurried towards the door. I could see the outline of two people through the frosted glass panel. One was big, one was small. Ebenezer Odd and Norman perhaps. I wasn't entirely convinced, but that didn't stop me from preparing for the worst.

My heart was pounding as the door handle began to rattle. Next thing, the door swung open ... and I exploded into life.

Taking aim, I threw an apple as hard as I could at the first head that appeared in the doorway.

I missed.

I tried again with a banana, but the result was the same. My aim was off. As a last resort, I tossed the entire bowl into the air, but it was too late. My legs had already turned to jelly. I was on my way down when two hands grabbed me around the waist, stopping me from falling.

'Are you okay, Hugo?' asked Poppy Wildheart. Which probably meant that the other person in the room was ...

'Don't be too nice to him!' barked the Big Cheese. 'He nearly took my moustache off flinging all that fruit about!'

'He's not well,' insisted Poppy, struggling to hold me up. 'Look at him.'

'Do I have to?' muttered the Big Cheese. 'I'm not overly fond of children at the best of times ...'

Poppy gasped for breath. 'Can you help me, sir?'

'What with?' asked the Big Cheese, looking over his shoulder.

'With Hugo,' Poppy moaned. 'We need to get him back to bed. He's too weak to walk there by himself.'

'He's weak?' blurted out the Big Cheese. 'What about

me? I didn't even get to finish my breakfast this morning. Well, my *second* breakfast. My first one didn't even touch the sides—'

'Sir,' pleaded Poppy.

'Okay,' sighed the Big Cheese. 'I'm not going anywhere near his armpits, though ...'

Somehow, against all odds, the two of them managed to carry me back to the bed and lay me down. My eyelids began to droop and I could easily have fallen asleep.

Not yet, though. Not until I had got some answers.

'What's going on?' I mumbled.

'We were hoping you might be able to tell us,' frowned the Big Cheese.

I gently shook my head. 'Where am I?'

'Hospital,' revealed Poppy. 'The Crooked Care Clinic to be precise. It's on the outskirts of Crooked Elbow. Not far from where you were found.'

I put a hand to my forehead, confused. 'No ... I thought ... Odd Island ...' I mumbled.

'Odd Island?' the Big Cheese boomed. 'What in the name of a badger's bottom is Odd Island?'

Poppy rested a hand on the Chief of SICK's shoulder. 'Hugo's been gone for four days, sir,' she said calmly. 'That's a long time for anybody, especially a young boy. Just give him a moment or two and I'm sure he'll tell us what he knows.'

She was right. I took several deep breaths, focussed my mind and then told them everything that had happened. And when I say everything, I mean everything. From child zappers to Mrs Snuggleflops via midnight treats and Isolation, I told them every last detail. If I forgot something I went back and filled in the gaps. I struggled when I reached my final day, though. I could still see Wheelie and Angel back in the hut ... Mo and Dodge as they led Norman in the wrong direction ... and Fatale curled up in a ball when the poisonous gas took its toll. She had insisted I leave her behind. And, against my better judgment, I had done just that. Once I had made her a promise, of course.

My memory went a little hazy after that. I had some kind of vague recollection of a wall with a door in it, bright lights and a horn, but it was all so blurry that I couldn't be sure that any of it was real.

By the time I had finished speaking, the Big Cheese and Poppy knew as much as me. It had been an exhausting experience, make no mistake. And I wasn't the only one who seemed to find it tiring.

'Sir,' said Poppy, nudging the Chief of SICK.

'Yes, dear,' the Big Cheese muttered. 'Six slices please. And lots of butter.'

'Sir,' repeated Poppy, nudging him again. 'Hugo has finished.'

'Has he?' The Big Cheese yawned before slowly opening his eyes. 'Thank goodness for that. That was quite some story. Very ... erm ... long-winded. For a moment there I thought I might even fall asleep—'

'You did fall asleep, sir,' said Poppy, shaking her head at him. 'I had to wake you. I'm not sure how much you missed, but Hugo has been through a terrible ordeal—'

'He's not the only one,' nodded the Big Cheese. 'I once got my head caught in a lavatory. Somebody else's lavatory as well. Don't ask me why, but I was searching for a pencil. What I found instead, however, was the stuff of nightmares …'

'This is much worse than that, sir,' remarked Poppy. 'Hugo could've been trapped on Odd Island for the rest of his life. We've been so worried about him, haven't we?'

'Well, *one* of us has,' shrugged the Big Cheese. 'I'll even give you a clue. It wasn't me. Right, young Dare, just tell me again. Did you find the children?'

'Yes, sir,' I said. 'I found them all. Every last one of them. With an extra dollop of Fatale De'Ath for good measure.' I stopped suddenly. 'I was supposed to rescue them,' I muttered under my breath.

'Yes, you were,' nodded the Big Cheese.

'Sir,' frowned Poppy. 'There's no need to—'

'I've failed,' I said honestly.

'Yes, you have,' agreed the Big Cheese.

'Sir,' said Poppy again. 'Please …'

'It's okay, Pops,' I said. 'He's right.'

'No, he's not,' argued Poppy. 'We can still go back to Odd Island and rescue the children. All you have to do is tell us how to get there.'

'That's the problem,' I said sadly. 'I don't know where it is. I couldn't find it even if you gave me a map. No, *two* maps. I haven't got a clue.'

The room fell silent.

'Then that's that then.' The Big Cheese sighed as if all the air had been sucked out of him. 'It's over. There's nothing we can do. The children are gone ... forever.'

That simple sentence stung me like a swarm of wasps with extra stinging powers. It wasn't over. It couldn't be.

Swinging my legs over the side of the bed, I tried to stand.

'Hugo, what are you doing?' asked Poppy, laying me back down again.

'What I should've done in the first place,' I replied. 'I'm going to rescue the children. And then I'm going to stop Ebenezer Odd once and for all.'

'And how are you possibly going to do that?' snorted the Big Cheese.

I rested my eyes. Suddenly I could see them. Back in the hut. Sat on their beds. Wheelie and Dodge. Mo and Angel. The Survivors. No, they were more than that. They were my friends. I had shown up on Odd Island, caused chaos at every opportunity and then left them behind. I had got out, but they were still there, suffering at the hands of Odd. The thought of it was enough to sicken me.

And what about Fatale De'Ath? I couldn't ignore the last thing she had said to me. *If just one of us gets out, we can all get out.* I repeated the words until they stuck in my head. Over and over and over again. There was no way I would forget it now. Not even if I wanted to.

'Are you still in the room, young Dare?' cried the Big Cheese. 'I asked you a question. How are you going to rescue the children and stop Ebenezer Odd once and for all?'

I opened my eyes. 'I'm going back to Odd Island,' I said defiantly, 'and this time I won't be coming home alone!'

The Big Cheese stared at me for a moment before throwing his hands up in the air and whooping with delight.

'I was hoping you would say that,' he bellowed. 'We're ready when you are, young Dare, but we haven't got long. Time is of the essence. Set your stopwatches because Operation Odd One Out is about to begin. Starting ... from ... now!'

THE END

HUGO DARE WILL RETURN

IN...

OPERATION ODD ONE OUT

OTHER BOOKS IN THE SERIES

THE GREATEST SPY WHO NEVER WAS (HUGO DARE BOOK 1)

Meet Hugo Dare. Schoolboy turned super spy. Both stupidly dangerous and dangerously stupid.

A robbery at the Bottle Bank. Diamond smuggling at the Pearly Gates Cemetery. The theft of priceless artefact, Coocamba's Idol. Hugo is there on each and every occasion. but then so, too, is someone else.

Wrinkles, the town of Crooked Elbow's oldest criminal mastermind.

In a battle of good versus evil, young versus old, ugly versus even uglier, there can only be one winner ... and it better be Hugo otherwise we're all in trouble!

THE WEASEL HAS LANDED
(HUGO DARE BOOK 2)

Schoolboy turned super spy Hugo Dare is back ... and this time he's going where others fear to tread!

No, not barefoot through a puddle of cat sick. This is much, much worse than that.

Maya, the Mayor of Crooked Elbow's daughter, is being held captive in one of the most dangerous places known to mankind.

Elbow's End.

Populated by rogues and wrong 'uns of the lowest order, only one person can find Maya and get her out of there in one piece. Unfortunately, that person is busy flossing their nostrils so it's left to someone else.

And that someone else is Hugo!

THE DAY OF THE RASCAL
(HUGO DARE BOOK 3)

Teenage super spy Hugo Dare returns. That's the good news. The bad news is he's faced with his perilous mission yet. We'll come to that in a moment …

The Day of the Rascal. A day when the whole of Crooked Elbow falls foul to the devilish antics of one devious little delinquent. The year, however, the Rascal has turned the screw. No more childish pranks and elaborate stunts for him. No, this year he plans to take out the Chief of SICK … and I don't mean for dinner! He wants to finish him off. Eliminate, eradicate and exterminate. RIP the Big Cheese.

Hugo is soon on the case. His instructions are simple. Stop the Rascal before it's too late. Easy-peasy. With any luck he might even be home in time for breakfast.

If only that was true …

THE HUNT FOR HUGO DARE
(HUGO DARE BOOK 4)

Schoolboy-turned-super spy Hugo Dare is used to danger. He lives it every day. Morning noon and night. Some might even say it's his middle name. (That's ridiculous. Who would ever say that?) This time, however, things are even more dangerous than ever.

Pursued at every turn by a wretched pack of undesirables, Hugo more use all his skills to shake them off and, ultimately, stay alive. It's anything but easy though, and with the streets of Crooked Elbow no longer safe, where can he go when everywhere spells trouble (not literally)? Who can he trust when he can't even trust himself (that's probably not true either)? And will he ever get the chance to ditch his school uniform for something a little more sophisticated (I'm guessing he will)?

The Hunt for Hugo Dare has begun … and only one young spy can make sure it doesn't end in disaster!

ACKNOWLEDGEMENTS

Thanks to the wonderful Sian Phillips for her eagle-eyed editing skills and glowing praise.

Thanks to the wonderful Stuart Bache and all the team at Books Covered for the front cover.

Thanks to everyone at the wonderful Polgarus Studio for their first-rate formatting.

Note to self – look for another word other than wonderful. Do not forget. Because that would be really embarrassing. I'm embarrassed enough already just thinking about it.

AUTHOR FACTFILE

NAME: David Codd. But you can call me David Codd. Because that's my name. Obviously.

DATE OF BIRTH: Sometime in the past. It's all a little hazy. I'm not entirely convinced I was even there if I'm being honest.

BIRTHPLACE: In a hospital. In Lincoln. In Lincolnshire. In England.

ADDRESS: No, thank you. I don't like the feel of the wind against my bare legs.

HEIGHT: Taller than a squirrel but shorter than a lamppost.

WEIGHT: What for?

OCCUPATION: Writing this. It doesn't just happen by accident. Or does it?

LIKES: Norwich City football club, running, desert boots, parsnips.

DISLIKES: Norwich City football club, running, rain, Brussels sprouts.

REASON FOR WRITING: My fingers needed some exercise. They were getting lazy, just hanging there, doing absolutely nothing.

ANYTHING ELSE: Thank you for reading this book. If you've got this far then you deserve a medal. Just don't ask me for one because I haven't got any. But I am very grateful. And do feel free to leave a review on Amazon if leaving reviews on Amazon is your kind of thing. It's not easy for a new author so please be kind.

Until the next time …